THE
DAMAGE

Copyright © 2014 by Amanda Moon
Previously Published as *Finding the Ruby Slippers*

Spiraling Forward Press
amanda@spiralingforward.com
www.spiralingforward.com

Ordering Information:
Quantity sales. Special discounts are available on quantity
purchases by corporations, associations, and others. For
details, contact the publisher at the address above.

Printed in the United States of America

ISBN
Softcover: 9781943250004
ePub: 9780990332671
Mobi: 9780990332688
1st Edition Softcover: 9780990332664

Second Edition
Cover Photo and Design by Amanda Michelle Moon

For Mom and Dad

THE

DAMAGE

AMANDA MICHELLE MOON

The cyclone had set the house down very gently—for a cyclone—in the midst of a country of marvelous beauty. There were lovely patches of greensward all about, with stately trees bearing rich and luscious fruits. Banks of gorgeous flowers were on every hand, and birds with rare and brilliant plumage sang and fluttered in the trees and bushes. A little way off was a small brook, rushing and sparkling along between green banks, and murmuring in a voice very grateful to a little girl who had lived so long on the dry, gray prairies.

—L. Frank Baum; TheWonderful Wizard of Oz

thesis, in which she presented a case against open-pit mining and for reopening abandoned underground mines, had been polarizing. ReEarth already held interests in open-pit mines, so it was entirely possible she'd gotten this job in spite of her work, rather than because of it.

He'd positioned them so the windows were behind her, placed a folder in front of her and flipped it open. She could still feel the sun on her back and relaxed into its warmth. "All of your paperwork is in there, including your copies of the non-disclosure agreement you signed. I'm glad you stayed here in Duluth. As I was saying, we've been watching your research into the copper and nickel deposits on the Iron Range. You obviously have a true understanding of the mining culture up here. It took a lot of guts to propose something so radical." He smiled again. "I really admire it."

She felt the knots in her stomach untying. Ben was as nice as he'd seemed in the interview and, with his blue eyes, quick smile, and slightly shaggy brown hair, incredibly attractive. She felt her cheeks getting warm and took a drink of her water. He was her boss, and she didn't want him to think she was getting the wrong idea.

"What I couldn't tell you during your interview was, everything you proposed, we're doing it. We're going underground, using existing mine shafts to extract the minerals that were left when everyone was focused on iron."

Ben's knees were bouncing under the table. Kelly wanted to speak, but was too shocked to say anything.

She was embarrassed that the first thoughts that went through her mind weren't all of the reasons this was amazing, but, instead, all of the reasons she'd been told it wouldn't work: The mines were full of water and unstable. Underground mining wasn't efficient. The permitting process was too hard. The public would never allow it.

"No. I know, right?" Ben's eyes danced. "It's really exciting. We've purchased our first mine and done preliminary drilling. The one we picked has been closed for nearly a hundred years now, so it was cheap, not a large risk if it didn't work out. But you were spot on in your thesis: the copper and nickel are here, and we can get to it using existing tunnels. Granted, there is a lot of work to do, both in the mines and in educating the public. Tomorrow, we're going in with reporters to check out the buildings, see the main shaft, show them what we're working with. The site is near Chisholm. Have you heard of Grace?"

She swallowed her recognition of the name and tried to keep her face placid.

He turned his laptop and showed her the point on the map. "This is just exploratory. Mostly for investors. It's not a large mine. But I want you there with the engineers tomorrow."

"I thought that property was privately held?" she asked. The mine had been owned by the grandparents of her best friend from childhood, Eric, but she'd been actively avoiding him for years.

"Oh, good! You're familiar with it. That's great. Yeah, a lot of people thought the mine was owned by the same people who owned the house beside it, but it wasn't. We bought it from the state a while back. We did get that house too, for next to nothing when the estate went up for auction."

Kelly swallowed the lump in her throat. If the estate was at auction, Eric's grandparents must have died. She hadn't talked to them since she'd cut off communication with Eric, but it was still a shock to hear they were gone.

"You okay?" Ben asked.

"Yeah, sorry." She nodded and rubbed her hands on the arm rests of her chair. "I was just remembering. I used to play in that mine when I was a kid."

"You what?"

"Well, you know, not *in the mine* in the mine, but in the shaft building. My best friend growing up—his grandparents owned the adjacent property."

"Oh, wow. That's incredible! That must have been back before they locked everything down, huh?"

Kelly forced herself to smile. "Well, it was locked, but we had our ways. Thinking about it now, though… if my kid was playing in a mine…" she shook her head. "We were stupid."

"Brave. Not stupid." Ben leaned close. "I used to build boats out of scrap wood, cardboard, foam, whatever I could find, and explore the creeks on our property. I'm lucky I didn't drown. I also didn't realize that every time I *lost* a boat and let it float down the creek, I was littering." He shrugged. "I feel bad sometimes that my girls won't ever get to have the same kind of adventures we did." He poured himself water from the pitcher in the middle of the table. "Wait. Did you know the kid that was killed over there?"

Kelly squeezed her eyes shut and nodded once.

"That whole year was weird. I think it was the same year the Ruby Slippers were stolen from that museum in Grand Rapids, then those kids were shot… That kind of stuff doesn't happen around here. It was crazy." He shook his head.

She swallowed. She knew it was her turn to speak, but was afraid of what might happen if she opened her mouth. The silence stretched out.

Right before it got awkward Ben asked, "You have kids?"

She inhaled deeply. Jordana she could talk about. "One. A girl. She's in kindergarten."

"We'll have to get the kids together sometime. My daughters are eight and ten."

"That'd be great. We're still getting settled in up here."

"You weren't here while you were in school?"

Kelly shook her head. "Grand Rapids. With my parents. They helped a lot with Jordana."

"Where are you living now?"

"An apartment in Hermantown."

"We're not far then—we're at the top of the hill, too. Let's set something up soon. We're meeting at the mine tomorrow at nine. You can ride with me if you want."

"Let me get back to you." She felt like he was flirting, but didn't know for sure. He didn't have a ring, and something told her he was a single father.

Regardless, she didn't want to risk starting something already, on her first day. She wasn't that girl anymore. Since Jordana was born, she had become cautious. And work was not the place to find a boyfriend. "I might be driving Jordana to Rapids to spend the weekend with my parents."

"No problem," Ben said. "My cell will be programmed into your phone when you get it later today. Give me a call in the morning if you want me to pick you up."

"Thanks." Kelly ran a hand through her hair, a nervous habit she was trying to break.

Ben nodded as he stood and started to the door. "Let me show you your office."

Kelly followed him on a short tour of the building, stopping at the offices that lined the outside walls and banks of cubicles in the center to be introduced to more people than she would ever remember. In general, the majority of the people in the center cubicles were women, with men in the offices. Kelly didn't take lightly that she was one of only a few women in a leadership role at any of the mining companies on the Range. She'd fought to get here, and was determined to prove herself.

"Here's the kitchen," Ben said, pushing open a door. A little further down the hall he showed her another room, the size of a walk-in closet with a table and four chairs in the center, and said, "Here's a small conference room with no windows, so if you need a place without a view..."

She smiled and shook her head. "I'm sure I'll be fine."

~~~~~

Kelly's office was sparse: a simple desk, one bookcase, and the wall of windows. A door opened into a small lab with rows of cabinets lining the walls, two worktables in the center, and a counter with a built-in sink.

"Get settled in, then go visit HR before you leave to be sure there isn't any more paperwork," Ben said. "Your computer is all set up. The Grace details and tomorrow's agenda should be in your email. Call me if you need anything. Kevin from IT should be up with your cell within an hour, but if you don't have it by lunch we'll hunt him down together." He held out his hand and said again, "I'm excited to have you here."

Her grip was firm. "Thank you. I'm happy to be here."

She wanted to explore the lab, make a list of what equipment was on hand and what she would need to order, but instead, she sat down at her desk, opened the laptop and began paging through the introductory emails from nearly everyone in the company. She'd just gotten to the first email about the Grace project when the IT guy came up with her new cell phone. Then someone from Human Resources instant messaged her and said they were missing some paperwork. When she was going back to her office, Ben met her in the hallway and insisted on taking her to lunch, where she learned that he had also gone to UMD and was indeed a single parent, but had a good relationship with his ex. He asked about Jordana's father, but Kelly deftly changed the subject by asking about his time at UMD. They'd been several years apart, but had some of the same teachers. By the time she got back to her office, she had just a few hours before she was scheduled to pick up Jordana.

She skimmed the information as quickly as she could. At the beginning the project was code-named *Moonlight Graham,* a reference to the portion of *Field of Dreams* that had been filmed in the same town as the mine. She liked the implication of destiny. Once they took this step—reopening an underground mine— there would be no going back.

~~~~~

Eric woke with the bed sheet tangled around his neck and covering his face. He struggled to push it off, but only pulled the noose tighter in the process. His temple was throbbing, the phantom pain he woke up with whenever he dreamt. He didn't remember much of the dreams, but somehow knew they were all the same. Darkness. A jet black Silverado. Cold.

The medication helped him go to sleep and kept him out, but he really wanted one that stopped the visions. Especially now that they were coming nearly every night. For a while he tried staying awake for days at a time, hoping pure exhaustion would keep the images at bay. But the terror still came, and the drugs made it harder to wake up.

His phone buzzed and he grabbed it from the nightstand, hoping to see *Joey* on the caller ID. Eric had been afraid he'd hallucinated the phone call with Joey in the hospital—he'd certainly hallucinated after it—and Joey had moved away so long ago, his involvement didn't even make sense. But a few weeks after Eric was home Joey had called again. With less medication and less pain Eric had been able to fully process it when Joey explained hiring Jared to steal the ruby slippers and arranging to sell them in New Orleans. The job was supposed to wipe both Joey and Jared's debts clean. As he described the guy they owed the money to, Eric knew immediately it was Charles. The gunshot seemed to be the only reason Joey believed that Eric didn't know where the shoes were.

"I've paid him off, but he's mad," Joey had said. "If he comes back…"

They agreed to keep tabs on one another, to watch out for Charles together. After that, Joey called to check in every six weeks for more than five years. There was no warning when they stopped, but when Eric tried Joey and the messages went unanswered, he knew what it meant: he was on his own. Fucked. Joey was gone and Charles was out there. That's when the dreams got really bad.

The phone rang again in his hand and pulled him back to reality. Sherrie's name was on the screen, not Joey's. He pressed the button and made himself smile. "Hi, buddy."

"Hi, Dad." Matthew's voice was often the first thing Eric heard in the morning and it usually calmed him. Sherrie had taken Matt to live with her parents when he was just a baby and Eric's panic attacks were especially uncontrollable, but she'd made a concerted effort to give Eric the opportunity to be involved on a daily basis, starting every morning with a quick phone call.

This morning, as Matthew talked about the Little League game he'd played the night before, Eric couldn't concentrate. The shaking and throbbing were getting worse, not better. He walked out to his tiny balcony, the phone between his shoulder and ear, and lit a cigarette, feeling the nicotine enter his blood stream, spread through his body and push out the dream. But neither the shaking nor the terrible feeling in the pit of his stomach would go away.

His eyes couldn't focus on the sunshine throwing shadows across the apartment complex's yard or the fluffy white clouds lazily floating by in the paint-blue sky. He didn't even notice the mosquitos landing on his arms and neck, stabbing him with their nose-spears.

"Hey, buddy?" he interrupted Matt. He didn't even know what the kid was talking about. "Can I talk to your mom for a minute?"

"Sure! I've got to get ready to go anyway. See you later!"

"Yeah," Eric said, wondering if *see you later* was a goodbye, or if he was supposed to be picking Matt up this afternoon. He couldn't shake the dread clouding his mind to remember or process what he needed to do today.

"Hi," Sherrie said. Eric could hear her moving around, dishes rattling together, floorboards squeaking. "I've only got a minute. I've got to drop him off and get to work."

Eric nodded. "Yeah. Sorry."

"You're still picking him up, right? I can't change that meeting."

"Um…"

"Did you forget?"

"No. I…Yeah," he admitted. "But I would have remembered. I'm having a hard time getting going this morning."

Her side of the line got quiet. "The dreams?"

"Yeah, but it's worse today. I feel like something bad…" it was the same thing he always said. He didn't know how to explain that this time it really was different.

"Eric. He's gone."

"That's the problem, though. We don't know. Just because he never went back for the truck…"

"Eric. The person who shot you is in jail. Remember? They busted the whole meth ring. No one is coming after you." She sighed. "I really wish you'd see someone. You need to talk to a professional about this."

Eric didn't answer, and she started to repeat the words that he'd heard so much during the first year: *You're lucky to be alive. If the bullet was a fraction of an inch over... You have to move on with your life. Don't let this haunt you.* "I've got to go. See you tonight."

He nodded, hung up, and took a long drag on the cigarette. In the shower, he ran the water as hot as he could stand, attempting to wash the dreams away. It didn't work. He needed to talk to Kelly. She would understand.

But he'd promised not to call her anymore.

~~~~~

Kelly had to use her GPS to find the road to the mine. When she and Eric had gone, they'd always started at his grandparents' house and run through the woods. Back then, all of the tiny country roads had been dirt. Now they were freshly paved, possibly a "gift" from ReEarth to the residents of the area. Also necessary for getting modern equipment in and out.

The building they'd played in, the surface entrance to the mine shaft, looked so much smaller than she remembered. Three concrete steps led to a new solid steel door. Broken windows had been boarded up. The building looked secure, almost ominous, in a way she'd never considered as a kid.

The dirt under her tires was red with iron oxide. Off to one side was a meadow bordered by woods, and though she couldn't see it, she knew there was a creek not far beyond the tree line. When she was a kid it took twenty minutes to run from here to Eric's Grandma's front door.

Kelly's was the third vehicle on site.

"Get your hard hat," Ben opened the door of his truck and called to her. He was wearing jeans and a blue button-down shirt, the cuffs rolled to his elbows, tie loose and top button undone. His steel-toe work boots looked like they'd saved his feet more than once.

She grabbed the hat and her bag, and wondered if she was over-dressed in her black slacks and blazer. Underneath, her purple silk shirt clung to her arms. On her feet were black boots with square one-inch heels. Not drastically different from the boots she normally wore in the field, just nicer. For some reason, she'd felt maybe she should be dressed for the occasion today.

"Sorry," Ben said, playfully thumping on her head as they walked together to the building. "No one likes 'em, but they're required. Even if the only thing that can fall on us is a tree."

Kelly looked at the tops of the evergreens hundreds of feet above their heads. "I don't mind. But I don't think this thing is going to do much good if one of those comes down."

He tilted his head and smiled. She could almost see his eyes through his sunglasses. Aviators, but not the mirrored kind, the cheaper kind you could buy at any department store.

Before she could decide whether to tell him that she was remembering how the building used to look or keep the conversation in strictly professional territory, the door of the other vehicle opened.

Kelly smiled as an older man, dressed similarly to Ben but without a tie, unfolded himself from the car, crossed the area between them and pulled her into a hug.

"I see you've already met Frank," Ben said.

Kelly smiled.

"I used to work with her dad," Frank said. "Road construction. We've been in touch over the years."

Kelly nodded. He'd called when Jared died and her name had first shown up in the papers. It seemed that all of Grand Rapids had a theory about the extent of her involvement in the theft and felt free to discuss it amongst themselves in voices loud enough for her to hear. Or point-blank ask her where the shoes were. Not Frank, though. When he'd asked her if she had anything to do with the theft, he'd accepted her answer when she said no and had never brought it up again.

There were only a handful of people who had seen her wear the shoes in the bar, but it was enough to spread it through the whole town. Lucky for her, no one had any proof, and the stories became part of the legend and rumor of the theft. The chatter had died down over the years, but she was glad not to be sending Jordana to school there, where the other kids might tell her God-knows-what.

"We're excited to have her here," Ben said, yanking Kelly out of her thoughts.

"Me too." Frank wasn't looking at them because he was already examining the building. "I'll tell you right now, that trestle needs to come down before we can have people working out here."

Kelly looked up at the arm-like protrusion coming from the side of the building. The railroad tracks that would have run underneath it were long gone, and the iron supports holding it up were rusted. But the most concerning issue was the multitude of holes through the metal and wood sides. It looked like a strong breeze could blow the whole thing over.

"Did you ever climb it?" Ben asked Kelly.

She shook her head. "We always stayed inside the building."

"You know this place?" Frank asked.

Kelly nodded. "My best friend's family used to own the land. Or they were the caretakers. I was never clear on that part. Anyway, their house was through the woods over there." She pointed in the general direction.

"Huh," Frank said. "I guess I didn't realize you knew the Stevenses."

"Their grandson was in my class," Kelly said. She was planning on changing the subject, but Frank nodded and began walking toward the building, asking Ben questions about the reporters.

"We've got some time," Ben said, "I've got the key if you want to go in."

Kelly and Frank exchanged a glance, nodded, and stood at the bottom of the stairs while Ben worked the old, rusty locks. When the door opened, sun shone onto the old metal stairs Kelly remembered so well. But the drop off the side seemed further. Forty feet was nothing to a kid without a worry in the world. Somewhere along the way she'd developed, among other concerns, a fear of heights.

Frank reached in, grabbed the pipe railing, and shook. The staircase rattled loudly, and Kelly thought she saw it move a little bit. "This isn't stable enough to have workers on," he said as he carefully stepped onto the metal- mesh platform. "It seems fine for one or two people at a time, but let's keep the reporters outside."

Ben nodded.

"I'm going down to take a quick look," Frank said. He turned to Kelly. "You coming?"

"Absolutely."

"Wait until I'm at the bottom."

Kelly nodded.

"Okay," he called up. "I'm clear. Is there a light in here?" Frank swept his flashlight over the long cracks running through the mortar of the cinderblock walls. The concrete floor was buckled, but everything was in relatively good shape for its age.

"Not that I know of. We always used flashlights." Kelly pushed the button on hers and a beam of light shot down the stairs. The tingling at the top of her spine that she'd been able to ignore while they were outside was growing into a rod of dread and spreading over her back. She took a deep breath and actively tried to keep herself from thinking about Eric and Brad, but with each step down the stairs her stomach seemed to get closer and closer to her throat. She swallowed hard and switched tactics, mentally cataloguing all of the repairs she expected Frank to submit. Major construction was needed. They wouldn't be back inside the mine for months. The more data she could collect today, the further along they'd be whenever the build-out was finished. At the base of the stairs she squeezed her eyes shut, forced all the air out of her lungs, and inhaled slowly. *Focus*. It wasn't until she stooped to dig a small dirt sample from one of the bigger holes in the concrete floor that she fully transitioned into work mode. She pulled a zip-top bag from her pocket, scribbled a note on the label, and slipped the sample inside. Finally mentally in work mode, she began walking toward the smaller tunnels.

Frank looked over from where he was examining the walls and corner joints. "Be careful back there. I'm sure it's wet."

"I will," Kelly said. She could hear running water, louder now than it was when she was a kid.

As soon as she left the main room, the cinderblock walls stopped and it became more of a dug out tunnel, supported on the sides by concrete, wood, and steel framing. The walls were higher here, but not much. It was cold, and she was thankful for her jacket as she began to carefully break away pieces of loose rock and slip them into labeled zippered bags. Her satchel was filling quickly and the weight of it was starting to pull on her shoulder.

It wasn't a conscious decision to skip the first two tunnels and enter the third, but as she shrugged her shoulder bag off, the shelf caught her eye and she realized where she was. Besides having a more powerful flashlight than she'd ever had as a kid, she was taller now. What she and Eric had always thought was just a short ledge was a much deeper crevice in the side of the wall—nearly two feet she guessed. It was completely empty except for a bunch of spider webs; everything they'd ever hidden there was gone.

She bent for a soil sample. A streak of red in the dirt caused her to fall backwards, slamming into the side wall of the narrow tunnel. Her flashlight spun and rolled until its beam pointed toward the entrance.

Eric had never said where in the mine he was shot.

She'd never thought about him being this far back, in their tunnel.

"You okay?" Frank called.

She tried to calm her breathing, to keep the tears from spilling over the corners of her eyes and keep her voice steady. How would she explain it if she came out crying? Faking claustrophobia wouldn't bode well for a career in mining. "Fine," she said. "I just tripped."

She took a few deep breaths, picked up the flashlight, and pointed it at the floor. The red streak was gone, but it came back when she changed the angle of the beam. It wasn't blood. Obviously. Her breathing returned to normal and she almost laughed at how ridiculous she was being, embarrassed something so basic had scared her so much. A six-year old bloodstain wouldn't be noticeable on rock, and it certainly wouldn't be red anymore. There was a tiny trickle coming from the side of the wall, ground water that had broken through.

As she picked up her bag, she looked one last time down the tunnel. At the very end of the flashlight's beam a metal square, covered in dust, blended almost perfectly into the background of dirt, dust and darkness. She put the satchel back down and walked to the lunchbox. Its cartoon sticker had faded and peeled, and she could tell by the weight it was probably empty. The metal-on-metal *ting* when she flipped the latch echoed through the tunnel, but the lid didn't open.

"Kelly! They're here!" Ben's voice, reverberating through the caves, seemed close and far away at the same time.

She didn't answer, just dug her fingernails between the top and bottom of the lunchbox to try to pry it open. The contract she and Eric made when they were ten years old, promising to be friends forever, might still be in there. Or any of the other random notes and pictures they'd felt were important enough to hide. When the lid finally gave the whole box flipped out of her hands and clattered to the floor. It was empty.

"Kelly!" Frank's voice was closer now. He was looking for her.

She took the box in one hand and her bag in the other and walked quickly back into the main tunnel where Frank was waiting.

"What's that?" Ben asked when she came out into the daylight.

She smiled, took her sunglasses out of her hair, and put them back on her face. "My treasure box. I left it there about twenty years ago."

~~~~~

There were a half dozen people from the media, all holding notebooks, cameras, or smartphones, standing in the grass outside the building. From his place at the top of the stairs, Ben quieted everyone, thanked them for coming, and launched into his prepared speech. "No one is doing underground mining anymore. These mines were closed when their iron stores were depleted. But there are huge reserves of copper and nickel all over the Iron Range. Our new technology will allow us to mine more efficiently, cleanly, and profitably *underground* with an environmental impact minuscule in comparison to open-pit mining.

"Now I get to introduce you to two members of our incredible team." He reached out and rested a hand on Kelly's shoulder. "Besides being top of her class and on the cutting edge of research, Kelly Martin was a mine rat when she was a kid." She watched the reporters take notes, smiled and raised her hand in a half-wave.

Ben's other hand went to Frank's shoulder. "And Frank Gustofsen is the best structural engineer on the Range. Safety of our workers is our biggest concern, and no one is better than him to ensure we do it right. As you can see from their clothes, they've already been inside. This project is underway!"

The three of them posed for a moment while cameras clicked, then Ben dropped his arms and asked for questions. Everyone wanted inside. Frank detailed the list of issues with the staircase alone, but couldn't appease the obviously disappointed crowd. Ben fielded whatever inquiries he could and deferred to Kelly and Frank whenever expertise was required. Kelly was nervous and kept her answers short, afraid she would say something against some ReEarth policy she wasn't aware of yet. Finally, reporters started packing up and drifting away. Ben's smile was huge as he shook hands and thanked each of them for coming.

"Did you get everything you need?" Ben asked when the last news vehicle was gone.

Kelly nodded. Frank was making notes but made a sound Kelly assumed was assent.

"You sure?" Ben was talking just to her. "You're not getting back in here for a while, based on the look on Frank's face."

"That's for sure," Frank said without looking up. "Shouldn't have let you in today."

The sides of Kelly's bag bulged cartoonishly by her feet. She'd love to go back in, but she probably wasn't going to get anything more useful until she could go deeper anyway. She kicked it lightly. "I've got it."

~~~~~

The lunchbox rattled in the backseat for the entire eighty-mile drive from Chisholm to Duluth, refusing to let Kelly forget it was there, but she still didn't know what to do when she pulled into the parking lot outside of ReEarth. Part of her felt like she should get it back to Eric, but she also had a strong urge to throw it out the window and pretend it didn't exist.

She knew it made her a bad friend, and maybe a bad person, but she didn't want to talk to him. At the end, right before she cut off communication completely, he was always trying to tell her about some guy named Charles, but he rarely made sense. She knew he'd had problems with hallucinations since the shooting and it freaked her out.

The breaking point, though, had been when Eric tried to tell her he'd taken Jared into the mine with the shoes. That's when she knew he was making things up to try to keep her close. Even if he was desperate, Jared wouldn't have allowed Eric to get involved with the shoes. Jared was too paranoid. And he'd hated Eric.

She moved the lunchbox to the trunk when she got her bag out and tried not to think about it while cataloguing all the samples she'd collected. There were several tests she'd need to run in the coming weeks, but before she could do that she needed historical data. On her way out, she knocked on Ben's doorframe and stuck her head inside. "I'm going to the Drill Core Library Monday morning, so I'll be in around noon," she said.

He was looking at his computer, typing, his brow drawn together and jaw set. She could see his teeth grinding and wished she had waited before speaking.

"Yeah, that's fine. See you then." His eyes were dark, the excitement she'd seen that morning at the mine was gone.

"You okay?"

He shook his head. "Just the stupid environmentalists. I mean, I'd be fine with them threatening me. I'm used to it. But when they say things about my family..." he shook his head. "I just wish they'd wait for us to actually release information instead of speculating how we're going to completely ruin the world." He blinked a few times. "Sorry, I shouldn't let it bother me. And I definitely shouldn't be unloading it on you. Go. Research. Do whatever it is you do that will make my job easier."

She wanted to know what exactly he meant by *threatening* and how serious it was. Although she'd heard stories of special interest groups sometimes using fear to try to intimidate mining companies, she'd never experienced it. But Ben was already concentrating on typing again, so she turned and left.

~~~~~

Despite how empty the apartment felt when she got home, Kelly was thankful for the weekend without Jordana to finish unpacking. She'd been so focused on making sure Jordana felt settled and at home, the girl's room was the only one that looked like anyone really lived there. For the most part, the furniture was all in the correct rooms, but had been positioned haphazardly. Boxes were strewn around the rest of the apartment, some in the right places, some not. A few had been opened. In the kitchen, several were partially emptied on the countertops during an abandoned attempt to make dinner.

She started in her own room, hanging her clothing. From there she unpacked the bathroom, went to the living room, positioned the furniture and hung up some pictures. By the time she got a beer out of the fridge and turned on the TV, it was late. The familiar voice of Glinda asking Dorothy whether she was a good witch or a bad witch filled the apartment. Kelly's heart jumped. She started to change the channel but couldn't stop herself from waiting for the moment: the first scene showing the ruby slippers on the shriveling feet of the Wicked Witch of the East. She was tempted to pause the movie, advance it frame by frame, and really get a good look. But she'd done it enough times to know it was pointless. The tiny distinctions that each pair of the costume shoes had were invisible on screen. It was only in real life that she could see the nuances. Like the differences in the bows and beading on the pair Jared had stolen. Had she not pointed them out, he never would have noticed. He wasn't that observant. And he didn't care.

Jordana had definitely inherited some of that obliviousness, but in a child it seemed more like trust than inattentiveness. When you told her something, she believed you. It was an innocence Kelly feared, but, at the same time, hoped her little girl would hold on to.

She changed the channel, found a marathon of an old sitcom, and finished her beer while unpacking the kitchen. She fell into bed completely exhausted, but the old dreams about Jared, flying houses, and wicked witches were back.

E ric didn't read the paper. He usually didn't even see it. The only reason he did that day was because the gas station attendant was too busy talking to her friend to let him buy his cigarettes and lottery ticket.

ReEarth to Reopen Grace Mine near Chisholm

ReEarth has announced it will begin underground operations at the site of the old Grace Mine as early as this fall. Kelly Martin, ReEarth's new geologist, says they have developed processes that will allow them to cleanly and efficiently extract minerals like copper and nickel that were not mined previously.

Before he could get any further, the cashier looked up. "Yeah?" The look on her face and the tone of her voice made it clear she considered his presence inconvenient.

He tossed the paper on the counter, pointed out the other items he needed, and paid. In the truck, he scratched the ticket—a loser, of course—scanned the article, and felt his heart rate increase. The cigarette he lit didn't calm him. He hadn't been planning on going anywhere, but he turned the truck south, toward his favorite bar/restaurant.

The dining room was mostly empty when he arrived and picked out his booth overlooking Pokegema Lake, but he knew it would fill up soon as families left church and headed out for Sunday lunch.

He was supposed to see Matt later in the day, and had promised Sherrie not to drink before they were together, so he hesitated for a moment when the waitress asked what he wanted to drink, then decided it would be fine since the visit wasn't for several hours.

The first Jack and Coke was salve on his nerves. He finished it in one long gulp then ordered a second. This one he sipped as he skimmed the article.

His breath caught in his throat as he read the description of the mine, how the property had been vacant for so many years before ReEarth bought it and the surrounding lots.

There is a residence near the mine, along with several barns and outbuildings. ReEarth hasn't announced plans for their use yet.

The article didn't mention anything about Eric's grandparents or their care of the mine property for so many years, or his cousin, who died right outside its door. It did talk a lot about science and Kelly's work at UMD. The whole piece came off as very pro-mine, pro-industry, and pro-jobs. There was a small sidebar with opposition, something about untested chemicals and groundwater contamination, but he didn't read it very closely. His eyes kept wandering back to Kelly's name.

There was no mention how far they'd already been in the mine. They would have had to report finding the Ruby Slippers. If they were still there. Unless the cops were withholding the information, hoping that knowing the mine was open would motivate whoever hid the shoes to come forward. Start asking questions.

But even if they were withholding information about the shoes, they would have to announce if they'd found a body. The fact that it wasn't mentioned proved what Eric had known all along: Charles had gotten out. He was still alive. It was only a matter of time before he came back.

The waitress brought Eric a drink he didn't remember ordering, but rather than sending it back, he thanked her and sipped it, promising himself this would be his last. He'd have a lot of water, take a shower, and brush his teeth before he met up with Sherrie and Matt. They'd never know.

There was only ice in his glass when he called the number he'd had memorized since elementary school.

"Hi, Mrs. Martin. This is Eric." He enunciated carefully, knowing he'd need to do the same later with Matt and Sherrie.

"Eric?" Kelly's mom's voice had remained as unchanged as the phone number.

"Eric Stevens. I was in Kelly's class—"

"Oh, Eric! Sorry! I didn't recognize your voice. Call me Susan. It's been so long. How are you? I saw your parents the other day…"

He listened to her rattle on about his parents and the restaurant where she and John had seen them, then answered a few questions about himself, Sherrie, and Matthew. He avoided talking about their separation and didn't correct her when she said something about watching your kids grow up.

"I think he's about the same age as Kelly's little girl, Jordana. Have you talked to her lately?"

"No, actually, that's why I was calling. I saw her in the paper."

"Oh, yes. We're really proud of all that. It's going to put so many people back to work…"

It took effort to maintain his concentration as she spoke. He wasn't listening to the words at all, just waiting for an opening. Finally, she paused, and he said, "Can I have Kelly's phone number? I'd love to talk to her about the mine. You know, my grandparents used to own it."

"Of course! And yes, I do remember. You kids used to have a lot of fun there. Playing inside that mine…I can't believe we let you do that. But you know, that's probably what gave Kelly the interest she has in mining. Oh, we're just so proud of her. Okay, you have a pen ready? Her number is 218-555-4729. I'm going to see her later today. Do you want me to tell her—?"

"Thanks," he said, and hung up before she could continue.

~~~~~

The restaurant was starting to fill up, but he ordered one more drink, bent over the table, and carefully pushed the buttons on his phone with shaking thumbs. He wasn't sure if the problem was too much liquor or too many nerves. Maybe both.

"Hello?"

"Hey, it's Eric."

"Hi, Eric," Kelly said.

"I saw you in the paper."

"Yeah?"

"Well, I didn't see you. I read about you."

"I knew what you meant." Their conversations had always been short, clipped and awkward since that summer. An unspoken pact: Don't say too much and you won't reveal too much.

There was a long pause, and then she blurted out, "I have your lunchbox."

Eric waited for her to say more, but the words hung in the silence. *I have your lunchbox.* Was it a threat? Was she working with the cops? Baiting him to say something that would tie him to the shoes?

And if she had the lunchbox, she'd been at least that far into the mine. She would know whether or not Charles was still there.

"It was empty," she added.

Eric remembered how he'd kicked it, confirmation he'd been in the right place, just before... "I know."

45

"What?"

"I know it was empty. I left it in there."

When she didn't reply, he asked, "Did you find anything else?"

"No."

He couldn't outright ask. Someone might hear him. Or maybe she was working with the cops and they were waiting for him to implicate himself. But, if there was a decomposing body... "How did it smell?"

~~~~~

When the phone rang Kelly had been getting ready to go to Grand Rapids to pick up Jordana and have dinner with her parents. She'd wanted to be back to the apartment early enough to show Jordana the box she'd found: toys they'd thought were lost, including Jordana's favorite stuffed monkey. Kelly couldn't wait to see how happy she'd be and hadn't thought to look at the caller ID before answering the phone. Now, as she sank down on the couch, she wished she had. She hadn't fully decided she was going to tell Eric about the lunchbox, it had just come out. Doing so had obviously been a mistake. This weird crypticness—she didn't have the energy to deal with it. "What?"

"How did it smell? Inside the mine?"

"It smelled like dirt. And water. But mostly dirt."

His voice dropped, it sounded like he was whispering through clenched teeth. "You know they never found him, right? I was wondering… hoping…maybe he'd gotten lost down there. I figured, you know…" He let out a long breath. "If he was decomposing…you might be able to smell him."

Kelly swallowed the vomit threatening to rise in her throat. She had to get off the phone. "Yeah. Probably. But there was nothing down there."

Present Day

Kelly made mental notes as she drove down the dirt path through the woods to Whiteside Mine. First, it really was time to buy a four-wheel drive. If it rained, the wheel ruts would fill with water, turn to mud, and suck her little car down. Second, she was making a list of everything that needed to be done before the press conference tomorrow. She couldn't remember how her team had gotten roped into helping Marketing, but she really didn't mind. Until now, the first day of operations at Grace had been the most exciting thing that had happened since she started at ReEarth and even that would pale in comparison to this. Whiteside was much bigger to begin with, had greater mineral stores, and, with Wanless and Woodbridge already connected to it underground, the expansion possibilities were beyond comparison.

Her six employees—four interns and two full-timers—had met at the office and carpooled. Kelly could have ridden with them, but it would have meant three people in the back seat of Mira's mini-van. No one wanted to do that for eighty miles. Instead, she'd left directly from her apartment and enjoyed the quiet drive. The six of them, all dressed basically the same in jeans, t-shirts and steel-toe boots, were standing in a circle, talking, when she pulled up. They should have been unloading the folding tables from the back of Mira's van and carrying them inside the old barn-like building behind the vehicles.

"What's the problem?" she asked as she got out of the car.

"We don't have a key," Mira said.

"Oh, for Pete's sake." Kelly fished a key ring out of her pocket. "How long have you been waiting?"

"We just got here. It's no big deal." Mira tilted her head back to get a drink of coffee and the morning sun filtered through her hair. Mira's hair was usually a mess, equally because it was naturally curly and unruly, and because, between working at ReEarth and raising two kids under the age of five, she just didn't have a lot of time to worry about it. It didn't help that she was constantly picking apart her ringlets and winding them around her finger while she worked.

Kelly almost commented on how good it looked, but stopped herself. She'd wasted enough of their time already this morning. "I'm sorry. I should have sent the keys with you guys."

Besides the two deadbolts and latch lock, there was a chain wrapped around the door-handles, secured by two padlocks. She'd been given a set of unmarked keys, so it took a while to match them to the correct locks, but she numbered them as she went to make it faster in the future. The doors were wooden, solid and heavy, with rusted hinges that had been put on backwards. They squealed when she finally pushed, but moved more freely than she'd expected, easily opening and wanting to swing shut again as soon as she let go.

While her team began unloading folding tables and chairs from the vehicles, Kelly went deep into the building looking for something to hold the doors open. The floor was dirt and scraggly grass that had grown where streaks of sunlight shone through cracks and knotholes in the wood siding. Dust and spiderwebs shimmered in the hazy light, but most of the room was dark or in shadow. Originally this was probably where miners had punched their timecards, maybe even took their lunch breaks. In one corner there were remnants of what Kelly assumed was, at one time, a wood-burning stove, but it was missing pieces. She wasn't surprised. The padlock and chains were relatively new additions to the door. Considering how easily the hinges gave, it hadn't been long since they'd been used. There was no way to know how many people had been in and out over the years. There was nothing to use for a doorstop, but it didn't matter. One of the interns had built a make-shift wedge from some tree branches and everything was loaded in.

Kelly gathered everyone into a quick meeting, told them she'd finish setting up herself, then sent them out to survey and collect samples. She'd be back onsite several dozen more times and it was good for the team, especially the interns, to get the experience on their own. They already knew how to unfold tables and chairs.

This press conference was an opportunity for the reporters to get an exclusive first look behind the scenes, to track through every part of this mine's reopening. If it went as well as ReEarth expected, even half as well as Grace had gone, ReEarth was planning on ramping up their timeline and reopening old mines all across the Iron Range in the next few years. The company was hoping that having documentation of the entire process, particularly from the media, would make both the permitting and public opinion portions, which could take years, go much faster in subsequent projects. Grace had taken almost six years—ReEarth was already four years into it when she'd started. So far, this had gone faster, but not much. Everyone always wanted to know exactly what was happening on site. Now they would. This picnic was the first step. Showing how they were going to reuse the old building would play well. Especially considering how trendy reclaimed wood was these days.

Kelly put the last folding chair in place as the doorstop, which had been slowly slipping, gave way completely and the doors swung closed. The sun had gone behind a cloud; darkness quickly consumed the room, save for tiny slivers of silver-gray light in the cracks. When she flicked on her phone's flashlight feature, a large dark lump against the wall behind the left door caught her attention. It would have been a good doorstop if it was a little smaller, but a rock that size would be too big to move. But maybe, she thought, as she picked her way around the tables and chairs toward it, if it was packed dirt, she could break it in half with her boot. As she got closer, instead of revealing the muted colors of rock, the flashlight showed darker blackness. When she was about five feet away, it became clear it was a backpack. Two steps later, she saw a zipper pull with chipped paint. A gasp caught in the back of her throat. She covered her mouth to keep it there and, holding her phone in front of her like a weapon, took one more step, even though she didn't need further confirmation.

It was Jared's backpack.

Her free hand reached out, almost involuntarily. She knew she shouldn't touch it, but she needed to know ... The backpack was the last place she'd seen the Ruby Slippers.

"Kelly? You in here?"

Kelly jumped backwards, stumbling, just before the door was shoved open. The sun had come out again creating a halo around Joel's head in the doorframe. He and Mira both seemed angelic a lot of the time. During the year the three of them had been together, they'd grown as a team and as friends. They challenged each other and were competitive in a friendly way that made them all better scientists, debating theories, questioning testing methods and conclusions, instinctively knowing when to push (and how hard) and when to back off. Their research was the reason ReEarth was thriving the way it was, and also why they needed the media to get on board with the company.

She stepped out of the shadow, hoping he couldn't see her trembling. "I'm here."

"We've got everything. Should we head back?"

"Really? That was fast."

"We couldn't get into the shaft. It was just surface analysis."

"Of course. But we need to get into the shaft."

"The engineers haven't vetted it yet. Remember? We have to wait for the reporters. So if it collapses, it'll fall on them." He smiled, but Kelly shook her head and pretended to be annoyed as she followed him out into the sun. It really did irk her that every part of this project was going to be monitored by a reporter or camera crew, but she'd reminded everyone *this will make everything easier in the future* so many times that it reflexively floated through her head.

"Yeah, I know," Joel said, like he was reading her thoughts. Mira joined them. They talked for a few minutes about the interns, then Kelly promised to follow them back.

"I've got a few calls to make," she said.

"Good luck with that." Joel looked at the sky. "There's no service up here."

"I've got two bars," Kelly lied, looking at her cell phone. "It should only take a few minutes. I'll be right behind you."

"Suit yourself."

She pretended to lock up the building and watched as everyone piled into the mini-van, thankful again she had chosen to drive herself. In her car she scrolled through email on her phone until they'd pulled away, typing quick answers and hitting send even though she knew the messages would sit in her outbox until she was closer to civilization. On another screen she made a note to check on the internet situation up here—it was something the engineers often left for last, but the sooner there was a signal, the better they'd be able to send data between people onsite and those back at the office in Duluth.

When the van's sound had completely died away, she got out of the car.

~~~~~

Whiteside had been closed since World War II, when the iron ore was depleted in most of the mines in Northern Minnesota. It was shuttered, like the others, and locks were put on existing buildings. Nature took over. Ground water, no longer diverted, filled in most of the shafts and created new ponds on the surface. White birch trunks grew up in long stripes surrounded by dark pine needles. The rust-red dirt and water made the leaves of the new grass and trees seem that much greener.

Kelly didn't notice any of it as she walked back to the barn doors. Her fingers trembled, and she had a hard time fitting the keys into the locks. It seemed to take hours before she was able to pull the chain off and push the door open far enough to slip through.

She'd pulled work gloves on while she was in the car and remembered to grab a real flashlight. Approaching the bag slowly, she nudged it with the toe of her boot, carefully. A tiny thump echoed in the empty building. Whatever was in it was solid. She pushed harder then, flipping it over as gently as she could in case anything was living under it. It would be a perfect place for snakes: cold and dark, and while she wasn't afraid, exactly, she didn't like being surprised.

The only marks were from her boots. Otherwise, the even coat of dust showed it hadn't been moved in a long time. She squatted down, propped the flashlight on the floor, and slowly pulled the zipper. Inside, black plastic, maybe a garbage bag, was wrapped around a shoebox and secured with several layers of clear packing tape, too thick to cut through with her fingernails or the dull keys in her pocket. There were scissors in her car, but she didn't get them. She didn't need visual confirmation of the obvious. The more she handled the bag, the more opportunity she had to connect herself with the crime. She'd worked for years to convince people that she'd had no idea what Jared had done. If she broke the seal...there was too much room for failure.

She zipped the backpack shut, pushed it back where she'd found it, then swept her boot over all the marks on the dirt floor.

Of course she would turn them in. There wasn't a question. But she needed to take time, be smart about it. Until then, she'd keep people out of the building. Say it was unsafe. By the time the engineers came out to prove her wrong, she'd have a plan.

~~~~~

"How was school?" Kelly asked as Jordana jumped in the back seat of the car.

"Fine. I got the part." There wasn't much excitement in her voice, but Jordana was such an even-keeled child the tiny hint of enthusiasm made Kelly turn to see her face.

"You did?"

"Yep," she beamed. "I'm going to be Dorothy."

Kelly had tried to keep Jordana from *The Wizard of Oz* and the possibility of anyone ever asking if her dad was "that guy who stole the Ruby Slippers." But Susan thought she was being paranoid and read Jordana the books anyway—the same ones she'd read Kelly as a toddler—and took Jordana to meet the characters during Grand Rapids' annual Judy Garland Festival. When she found out about the play, Jordana had begged to be allowed to audition and spent weeks studying the movie, practicing songs and lines over and over. Kelly didn't have the heart to say no. But she didn't think they'd give the leading role to someone so young.

"That's awesome, sweetie!" Kelly wanted to be excited for her daughter, but as she pulled away from the curb her stomach settled into a hard lump at the bottom of her abdomen and her knuckles turned white on the steering wheel. "What do we need to do?"

"Practice my lines. It's not the same as the movie, and they say I have to learn what's written for the play instead of saying what Dorothy actually says. And I have to make my own ruby slippers. The shoes they have are way too big for me, I can't walk in them."

Kelly was grinding her jaw with such force she could feel it in the roots of her teeth. Recreating the ruby slippers would be easy. No one could accuse her of anything, just because the shoes might look too realistic. All it took was high heels, sequins, and glass beads.

Part of the reason she'd been excited about the job at ReEarth and moving to Duluth was the opportunity to blend in, start over. Still, the shoes had managed to catch up with both of them, and in the same day.

~~~~~

Kelly wished she could pick up the phone, call the number on the reward website, and collect the quarter million dollars that had been promised to anyone with information leading to the shoes' recovery. With that kind of money, she could set Jordana up for college, buy a house, pay off her own student loans…But it was impossible. She'd been questioned so many times and always said the same things: Jared told her he took the shoes (true) she thought he was lying (false) because he'd lied about most everything else in their relationship (true) and she had no reason to believe he had either the desire or means to carry out the crime (mostly true, she had no reason to believe it other than having seen the evidence.) If she suddenly showed up with the shoes, she'd be accused of having them the whole time and arrested on the spot. There was no way to prove she didn't. *I just found them behind the door of this mine I'm working at up by Buhl.* It didn't matter whether or not it was true—it was unbelievable even in her own head.

When they got in the house, Jordana dropped her bag in the middle of the floor, ran to the DVDs, and searched until she found *The Wizard of Oz.* A moment later the opening credits were playing.

"You don't need to watch that right now," Kelly said.

"Yes, I need to research my part," Jordana replied. "And you need to get a good look at the shoes in action. I want the pair we make to be perfect."

Kelly didn't have the energy to argue, even when Jordana went to the computer and began pinning images of the shoes for future reference.

Later, when the movie was paused and they were eating dinner at the table, Jordana asked, "Did you live in Grand Rapids when the Ruby Slippers were stolen?"

Kelly looked at her daughter, seeing so much of Jared in her eyes, nose and cheekbones, and tried to decide how to answer and where this question was going to lead. No matter what she did now, at some point Jordana would find out the truth. She nodded slowly.

"Where do you think they are now?"

"Buried somewhere, probably." It was one of the two most common theories. The other was that they were at the bottom of the Mississippi River. If Jordana ever repeated what she'd heard, no one would think anything of it. And it wasn't exactly a lie. The shoes were buried—under dust.

"Do you think they'll ever find them?"

Kelly sighed, picked up her plate, and carried it to the sink. "I hope so."

Jordana cleared the rest of the table quietly, obviously deep in thought, then went back to the movie.

While Kelly cleaned the kitchen and prepared their lunches for the next day, she made a plan. She'd do the same thing Jared had done; she'd go to the museum in the middle of the night. There were still no cameras. She could leave the shoes in a box by the door for the employees to find in the morning. She'd take the whole backpack and just leave it. No one would ever know where it came from.

"Hey, mom? Did you know no one really knows how long fingerprint and DNA evidence can last? This says it could be up to millions of years."

Kelly froze, forced herself to take a deep breath and steer the conversation away from the shoes. "Not exactly. But do you remember that dinosaur movie? *Jurassic Park?*"

"It wasn't real," Jordana said.

"But it was based on real scientific theory." Kelly walked into the living room so she could see what Jordana was looking at.

"Maybe, but listen to this: They've used forty-year-old fingerprints in court cases."

Kelly read over her daughter's shoulder about fingerprint and DNA evidence on the *South Dakota Division of Criminal Investigation* website, of all places. The knot in her stomach solidified into granite as the implications fully registered. She couldn't even find the words to ask Jordana how she found the site, or tell her to close the computer and get ready for bed.

"So, maybe," Jordana said, grabbing Kelly's hand, "when they do find the shoes, there will be fingerprints to tell who took them!"

~~~~~

Mrs. McAlester lived across the hall and had practically adopted Kelly and Jordana when they moved in. She brought over some sort of homemade treat nearly every day the first week: cookies, brownies, banana bread and more. Of her sixteen grandkids, three were near Jordana's age, and they were her first friends "in the building." On the rare occasion Kelly needed to leave for work before Jordana got on the bus, Mrs. McAlester was always willing to come over and stay with her. Kelly felt bad any time she had to ask, but was constantly assured *I get up at five-thirty. As long as it's later than that, it's really no trouble for me to come to your apartment and sip my tea. Jordana is such a sweet girl.*

When Kelly answered the door at six, Mrs. McAlester was holding a plate of cinnamon rolls, dressed in pleated blue slacks with a gray cardigan over her green t-shirt. "I hope you don't mind," she whispered, silently setting the plate down on the kitchen counter. "I woke up early today, so I made treats." She handed Kelly a warm cube of tinfoil, gave her a quick hug, and ushered her out.

A little over an hour later Kelly was standing in the driveway at Whiteside, the sun already above the trees and burning away a thin morning fog. She'd grabbed a large rock from the side of the gravel road on the way in and used it to prop the door open wide enough to block the backpack while she hauled the tables and chairs outside. Then she forced herself to pretend it wasn't there as she closed and relocked the doors. By the time Mira's van arrived, Kelly was sipping coffee at the new picnic area she'd set up.

"What's going on?" Ben was out of the passenger seat before Mira had even turned her van off.

"We're not going to be able to go inside today," Kelly said. "There's stability issues. I don't want a swift wind to blow the building down on a bunch of reporters. It won't help our cause at all."

Ben was looking at the building. "It looks fine to me."

"I thought it was okay yesterday," Mira agreed, squinting, her head cocked sideways, trying to see behind Kelly's eyes.

Kelly raised her eyebrows, hoping Mira could hear her telepathically pleading, *Trust me.*

"If Kelly has a feeling, I trust her," Joel said. "She's got good intuition."

Ben nodded. "I know. I hired her."

"Why didn't you at least let us help move this stuff out?" Joel asked.

Kelly shrugged. "I got here earlier than I expected, and you guys did it all yesterday. It wasn't a problem. Besides, I've done all my heavy lifting for the day. Now I'll supervise while you set up the food."

Ben laughed. "Yeah, right."

Mira pressed a button on her key ring and the back of her van opened slowly, revealing trays of sandwiches, bags of chips, paper plates and plastic cups. There were two-liter bottles of just about every kind of pop in existence and coolers full of ice. The breeze was light, but enough that they needed to use rocks to hold down the edges of the plastic tablecloths and stacks of napkins. Kelly tried to concentrate on the questions she was being asked, to engage fully in the conversations they were having, but her mind was divided. Since she'd first seen them, back in Jared's apartment, she'd felt magnetically drawn to the Ruby Slippers. Now they were so close. It took most of her concentration not to stare at the barn, where she imagined she could still see the outline of the backpack through cracks in the siding.

~~~~~

"The experience we've gained from Grace is the biggest difference between this project and that. Besides, of course, the size." Kelly smiled and cameras flashed. "We're constantly refining our methods to increase efficiency while always maintaining our focus on environmentally safe mining. We will continue our commitment to leave the area as good as or better than we found it." Her brown hair tumbled down the back of her crisp white shirt in perfect waves as she tilted her head back and took a long drink from her water bottle. She'd brought the clothes in a garment bag and changed behind the barn before the reporters arrived. It was an extra blessing when most of the dust and dirt had brushed easily out of her hair and she didn't have to keep the hard hat on during the press conference.

"Sorry about that," Kelly said, turning back to the reporters. "It's hot out here." The audience laughed politely, many fanning notebooks or pamphlets in front of their faces. "What I was saying," Kelly continued, "is that we do have a commitment to what this area will be like when we are no longer here. The majority of the mine is underground, nearly eliminating the surface footprint. With our technology, we plan to be operational for the next hundred years or more, providing jobs and economic vitality for generations. We are looking forward to continuing to expand. Ben's going to say a few words, then we'll take questions over lunch."

Ben had brought extra clothes too, but the heat was getting to him. His yellow tie had been loosened, and his blue shirt was open at the collar and the sleeves rolled up. Sweat glistened on his forearms and clavicle. The entire top portion of his face was obscured by a ReEarth baseball hat and sunglasses. He placed a hand lightly on her lower back as Kelly stepped away from the podium. "The one thing Kelly didn't mention, I guess because of her modesty, but, really, it's the most exciting part of the project, is the real scope of Whiteside compared to Grace. There, we are only on two underground levels. Here, we're planning to use the whole shaft, all of the previous tunnels, everything. Kelly's team, working closely with our engineers, has created processes to get deeper, create less waste, and exponentially increase yield. We are creating a new model in mine reclamation here, and it is exciting."

Kelly's mouth dropped open. She could tell by the way his cheek wrinkled up he was winking at her, even though she couldn't see his eyes. They weren't supposed to announce the full scope for several more weeks because she didn't have all of the environmental reports ready. And there were still stability issues that needed to be addressed.

The crowd was silent, absorbing the information. She couldn't tell if they thought it was good or bad. It really depended on what they understood of the mining processes and how they felt about mining in the first place; if they were worried about the environmental impact, the news would not be welcome. If they were excited about jobs…she would find out at lunch.

~~~~~

The event lasted longer than anyone anticipated. Ben's announcement had led to nearly an hour of questions before Joel was able to wrangle everyone to the tables by threatening that the food was going bad. The reporters, surprisingly, didn't seem to mind that no one could answer all their questions yet. Just the potential—it was something people had always hoped for, a return to the boom of the mining era—but no one had ever thought it was really possible.

Ben caught up with Kelly while she was gathering up the trash. "We need to talk."

"We certainly do."

He looked past her to the barn. "I wanted our offices out here," he said. "It's such a cool building. Do you think we can stabilize it?"

Kelly pretended to study it, letting all of the other, more important things they needed to talk about filter through her head before she opened her mouth. "Yeah, it'll just take some TLC."

He nodded. "Want to grab dinner tonight? We've got other things to discuss."

She shook her head. "I'd love to, but I have plans with Jordana."

His blue eyes were locked into hers. "Tomorrow then? Lunch?"

She nodded. "Absolutely."

~~~~~

Making ruby slippers for the play was harder than they had anticipated. First, the pumps Kelly and Jordana had bought had to be covered with pantyhose to create a netting that the sequins could adhere to. Then they had to run a very thin layer of glue and press each individual sequin into position. Tedious was an understatement. They'd been working for several hours when the local news came on, and Jordana went to bed only after making Kelly promise to finish so the glue could dry overnight.

After she tucked Jordana in, Kelly poured herself a glass of wine, clasped her hands behind her back to stretch her tight shoulders, and was getting ready to grab a fresh roll of sequins when the news came back on. Her own image filled the screen, sun gleaming in the background, and her voice: *"The majority of the mine is underground, nearly eliminating the surface footprint. With our technology, we plan to be operational for the next hundred years or more, providing jobs and economic vitality for generations."* The contrast between her poise and the next clip, an activist from the Twin Cities area, was stark, Kelly had actual science, the activist began almost every thought with "What if."

When the picture cut back to the newsroom, the anchors talked enthusiastically about the mine's incredible potential.

Kelly knew it was pretty much the best reaction ReEarth could have hoped for, and smiled as she changed the channel.

She'd had a lot of time to think about her options— it had been nearly two weeks since she first found the backpack—but still hadn't decided what to do when she arrived at Whiteside. She'd already rescheduled this meeting with Frank four times. When she tried again this morning he'd said he couldn't wait any longer and would go check out the stability of the barn without her. She couldn't let that happen. What if he found the shoes and turned them in? And even if he didn't, the building would eventually either be used or torn down, and they'd be found or destroyed. If what Jordana had said about fingerprints was true, Kelly's prints might still be on them. Plus, people knew she'd been at the site and even in the barn. They'd say she hid them there.

She couldn't let that happen. They had to be moved.

She'd turn them in, but not yet. If the shoes showed up now, just before the Judy Garland Festival, there would be way too much media coverage, it would easily attract national attention. There would be special events. No one would accept that they were back without asking questions.

But she didn't want to take them.

There were two other small buildings at the mine site, and she spent precious time examining each, trying to determine if she could move the backpack. Unfortunately, both were too close to the road and would be bulldozed as soon as ReEarth had the permits to begin expanding it, which could happen in the next few weeks. Hiding them in the woods was out. Too much risk of damage. Inside the barn they'd been semi-protected from the elements. The extreme heat and cold had probably been hard on them, but at least there wasn't rain and snow. She assumed they were more or less intact. She was responsible for them now, and keeping them safe was a priority.

Her phone buzzed, a text from Frank. *15 min out.* There was no way to know for sure if he'd just sent it, or if the spotty signal had just delivered it.

It was now or never.

She'd bought a gray rubber storage bin that morning and carried it with her to the barn. One of the locks stuck, and she could hear the far-off sound of an engine by the time the door screeched open. She ran in, grabbed the bag by the handle, and plopped it, too hard, into the bin, then rushed the whole thing to her car. Frank was rounding the corner as she closed the trunk.

"You already in there?"

She saw the door hadn't closed behind her, and the keys were still hanging from the lock. "Yeah, looking for something to block the door open for you."

He nodded and grabbed a flashlight. "It'll be fine. If you're concerned about stability you shouldn't be going in. Especially without a hard hat." He put his on and waited while she pulled hers out of the back seat, a distinctly parental look on his face.

"I didn't want it to fall down on you," she said.

When he didn't smile, she tried again.

"I don't think there's imminent danger or anything."

"Even if you just had a feeling, you have to trust it. Especially as a woman."

She knew he meant it as a compliment, but she still cringed.

"Show me what you saw."

Inside the building she shone her flashlight into a corner where water damage sagged the ceiling and ran in a line down the wall, then pointed out half a dozen loose boards. None of it was enough to make the building actually unstable, but it was at least something.

Frank walked first to the corner with water damage. He took pictures on his phone, examined corner supports, and poked at the ceiling with what looked like a retractable police baton. Kelly followed quietly as he examined the rest of the building, snapping photos, pressing on boards.

"Got it," he said, eventually. "Let's go check out the shaft."

She nodded and was locking the door when his phone chimed.

"Hello?" He looked at her, then walked a few feet away.

She felt her stomach fall to her feet. Somehow, someone found out. And they were coming for her. She swallowed and tried to remain calm, but her hands were shaking and she couldn't get the deadbolt to slide into place.

"Uh huh," Frank said. "Okay. It's fine. We can come back."

He turned back to her and she saw something register on his face. "You okay?"

She blinked quickly and slipped her sunglasses in front of her eyes. She couldn't speak, so she nodded.

Frank cocked his head, but didn't press. "That was Ben. There's a problem with the permit, we can't go into the shaft. We're done here. Want to grab lunch?"

~~~~~

Kelly could feel the presence of the shoes in the car with her, like a ghost sitting in the back seat. Or a hitchhiker who might pull a knife at any moment.

She found some music on her phone, plugged it in, rolled the windows down and cranked the volume up until she couldn't hear her own thoughts over the noise.

The diner Frank pulled into was one of his favorite spots. He'd taken her there before and Kelly didn't love it—almost everything on the menu was fried or covered in gravy—but she liked the crowd: mostly older men, nearing or enjoying retirement, full of great stories. Usually they sat at the little counter and Kelly listened while Frank and the other guys talked, but today he led her to a table in the corner, as far away from the other patrons as possible, and waited until the waitress had walked away before asking, "What's going on?"

She tilted her head, trying to figure out what she'd given away and what she could say that would satisfy his paternal instincts.

He spoke before she could decide. "There's nothing wrong with that building. It's old. Needs some reinforcements. That's it." He took a long drink of his pop without taking his eyes off her.

She shrugged and looked away. "Sorry. I guess, maybe because of the dark...I didn't have my flashlight..."

"Bullshit. You've been off lately."

She inventoried her actions. What could he have picked up on? She'd been working hard, as usual. Her team was running great.

"Is it the stuff with the shoes? Did you see it on the news again?"

Her eyes shot up to his.

"Guess not. Sorry."

"Why? What was on the news?"

Frank shook his head. She thought he wasn't going to answer and was about to ask again when he shrugged and said, "They ran a story—fluff piece, I guess they needed something to fill space."

"About what?"

"Just rehashing old information. Mentioned that Jared guy again." He broke eye contact to take a long drink of pop. She looked out the window at the car. It felt like the shoes were watching her.

"He's Jordana's daddy, isn't he?"

Frank's question brought Kelly immediately back to the conversation. The only people that knew were her parents. Even the cops—other than the one at Jared's apartment, no one had ever asked her again.

"You don't have to answer," he said. "I could see it as soon as they showed his picture on TV. She looks a lot like you, but she's got a lot of him in her too."

She had no idea what to say. After a long drink of water, she finally asked, "Why did they show his picture?"

Frank shrugged. "Needed to fill time or something. Don't worry. It's okay. I won't tell anybody. But we do need to talk about that building. Why did you think it was unstable?"

She wanted to tell him everything and ask for help. Maybe he would take the shoes himself, turn them in. He could say he found them. No one even had to know she was involved at all.

Except it would still come back to her. As soon as the media found out she and Frank worked together.

The theft would get pinned on her and he'd be deemed an accomplice. They'd both end up in jail.

"I mean what I said," he interrupted her thoughts. "You've got to trust your intuition. I'll trust it, too, if you'll tell me what you saw."

He was quiet then, waiting. Kelly sipped her coffee and shrugged, doing her best to make her expression and voice portray indifference. "There wasn't anything specific. I guess it was the sagging roof and that water damage. It was windy that day—it was coming in through the boards and kind of loud."

Frank nodded. "Personally, I think they should knock the whole damn thing down and build something new. But that's not going to happen. Everyone wants to leave that *natural* look, but they won't like it too much in the winter when the snow blows right inside. It needs a new roof before we get too many people in there. Then we'll pour a cement foundation, frame out the inside and insulate it. If they want that old wood look on the inside, they're going to need to get paneling."

Kelly scrunched her top lip and nose together and shook her head.

"What?"

"I hate wood paneling."

"Fine. Whatever. But no one is going to recognize the place when we're done."

"Then why aren't we knocking it down?"

"Sustainability, of course. Also known as: spending too much money for old shit that will continue to need money poured into it."

Kelly smiled and shook her head. She actually understood many of the environmental concerns of mining, it was one of the reasons she had gotten into the industry in the first place. But stuff like this…it didn't make sense. "What did Ben say when he called?"

"Not much. The permits didn't come through, but he didn't say why."

"He say when he expected them?"

Frank shook his head and looked up at the waitress approaching with two plates of food. "Nope. And you know what that means."

~~~~~

As proud as she was of her daughter, Kelly couldn't wait for *The Songs of Oz* performance to be over so she wouldn't have to hear "The Lollipop Guild" or "Ding-Dong! The Witch is Dead!" every day. Even "Somewhere over the Rainbow," in which Jordana had a solo, was starting to wear on her. Listening to her practice, Kelly wondered if Jared had been able to sing. She'd never heard him, but Jordana certainly hadn't gotten her ability from the Martin side of the family.

Kelly was one of the first parents to the auditorium and dropped her coat on a seat in the front row before going backstage to find Jordana. Most of the kids were indistinguishable, dressed as munchkins and Emerald City residents, but Jordana stood out in her white and blue jumper. She was helping the director sculpt a little boy's hair into a point on the crown of his head. Kelly had to wait until they were sure it was set before she could pull Jordana into a hug.

"You look great," Kelly said. A bit of Jordana's stage makeup rubbed off onto Kelly's cotton shirt, but she didn't care. She was thankful for the visual confirmation of her daughter's safety and happiness. It was all that mattered in the world. And the shoes, still locked in the trunk of the car, had the potential to completely ruin everything. Speaking of…she noticed Jordana's socks. "Where are your shoes?"

Jordana pointed to a dark corner. "Over there. They're too uncomfortable. I'll put them on right before I go out."

"I'm sorry."

Jordana shook her head. "I don't like high heels."

Kelly smiled. She wasn't ready for Jordana to grow up yet, and this proof that she was still a little girl was hands down the best thing that had happened all day.

~~~~~

Kelly nodded and thanked people as they told her how amazing Jordana's performance was. She could easily talk about her awesome daughter. But she felt her expression grow stony as people talked about the shoes, how realistic they looked, and asked if she'd ever seen the real shoes when they were in Grand Rapids. She tried to smile and told them about the tutorial Jordana had found online. The tension built between her shoulder blades as she waited for someone to put two and two together, remember her from that newscast way back when. She should have screwed up the details more. Not used sequins. Dipped them in red glitter. Something.

Jordana came out with makeup stuck in her hairspray stiffened bangs, the costume and shoes overwhelming her small arms. "Can we go get ice cream? Everyone's going."

Kelly agreed and took the bundle, then watched Jordana run off to find her friends.

The combination of adrenaline and sugar had Jordana bouncing off the walls by the time they got home, but after a hot shower she was practically asleep before Kelly finished combing the knots out of her hair.

Kelly turned on the late news, poured herself a glass of wine and sat down on the couch. She was trying not to think about the shoes in her trunk, but her mind couldn't seem to grab on to anything else.

Until the picture of the museum filled the screen.

"We reported last night about preparations for this year's Judy Garland Festival, and the continued investigation into the missing Ruby Slippers."

The picture changed to a pair of red shoes, with a big *Who Stole the Ruby Slippers?* sign underneath them. She wondered if this was the story Frank had seen, and why they were repeating it.

"The shoes on display now are replicas, holding the place of the original, movie-worn shoes that were stolen in 2005. Although it is widely believed that Jared Canning was the culprit, the shoes have never been found. Canning died shortly after the theft and never commented on the accusations, although he did contact the museum for ransom."

Kelly held her breath as a snapshot of Jared looking like the boy next door, not his mugshot, filled the screen. Jordana really did look a lot like him.

"A single sequin was the only evidence recovered from the crime scene. But tonight we have new developments."

Kelly jumped up.

"McDonald Investigations, a private firm out of Chicago, has joined the case. They are working independently, but with cooperation of the Grand Rapids Police Department. If you have any information, you are asked to call and leave a message at the station. The firm is not releasing the names of any specific investigators; however, they have released this statement: 'We will be combing through old police files and conducting interviews. Based on what we've seen so far, we're optimistic the shoes will be recovered.'"

Kelly put her wine glass down on the coffee table and looked at her cell phone, expecting it to ring immediately. The case was usually reviewed around this time every year, and she was often contacted by overzealous rookies sure they'd be the one to find the missing link. She tried to reassure herself that this was the same thing. There was really nothing to worry about. But she'd never had to lie about the location of the shoes before, because she'd never known. Now, she had them in her car.

~~~~~

The case of the missing Ruby Slippers has been turned over to McDonald Investigations from Chicago, Illinois. A provided statement withholds specific investigator names, but says they are joining the case as "fans of the movie, and avid collectors" with the goal "to see the shoes returned." The statement concludes: "We appreciate the opportunity to help bring closure to a community that has done so much to support Judy and her legacy." Grand Rapids police have confirmed they will be sharing case files with an outside agency but have declined further comment.

The article was on the upper-right corner of the paper with a small stock picture of the *Who Stole the Ruby Slippers?* sign that had greeted Grand Rapids visitors for years. Eric was relieved, there was no comment from the museum, the insurance company, or the shoes' original owner. It couldn't be a big deal.

He wondered how long it would be before he got a call, if this guy would finally be the one to actually link the fact that he was shot a little more than a week after the shoes were taken, in a remote area where Jared had been just days before asking the museum for ransom.

At the time, Eric didn't think he could ever be connected to the crime. That's why he'd helped. Staying close to Jared meant staying close to Kelly, which definitely wasn't a bad thing. And it was just plain exciting. Nothing ever happened around here. He'd talked about stealing the shoes so many times himself—just for shits and giggles, of course—to know the guy that actually did it...he couldn't let it go without trying to get in on the action. It would be a great story to tell to tell his kids someday.

Except now that he actually had a kid, all he wanted to do was make sure there was no way anyone ever figured out he was involved.

Every year around this time they said they were closer to finding the shoes, and asked for the public's help. But, so far, no investigator had ever asked him anything to make him think they were at all on the right track. Thankfully.

Not that it mattered. He had no idea where the shoes were.

He thought about it a lot the first few years. He told his grandparents he was helping clean up Brad's stuff and went through all of their garages. He visited Brad's ex-girlfriend's house and ended up sitting with her on the porch for nearly an hour while she cried over the man she'd said she hated on multiple occasions. He checked Brad's favorite bars, even his deer stand. There was no sign of the shoes anywhere. Not even a sequin. If Brad had handled them, there would have been something somewhere. The sequins dropped like Hansel and Gretel's breadcrumbs. But Eric was never able to find the trail.

The fact that a PI was investigating the case voluntarily didn't surprise him all that much. People were obsessed with the shoes, for one reason or another. Someone was always coming up with a new theory of what happened. Television shows and documentary movies had been made about the theft. No one could believe they were really gone. Someone, somewhere, had to know where they were. But no one was talking.

*H*i, Kelly, this is Mark McDonald. I have taken over the investigation into the theft of the Ruby Slippers. I have a few questions for you, if you wouldn't mind calling me back. My phone number is 218-555-7639."

Kelly let the voicemail play. She didn't delete it, but she had no intention of calling him back. He wasn't the police, so she was under no obligation to speak to him. He couldn't subpoena her. The more she talked, the more opportunity she had to implicate herself. Not even by actually saying something about the shoes, just by contradicting something she'd said in earlier interviews. It had been a long time. She wasn't willing to take the risk.

She kept the message so she'd remember the number, and make sure not to answer any calls from it.

~~~~~

The next message was left on her work phone. *"Hi, Kelly, this is Mark McDonald. I am a private investigator working on the Ruby Slippers case. I left a message on your cell phone, but in case that wasn't a current number, I hope you don't mind me leaving a message here, also. I'm working with the Grand Rapids Police Department, the Judy Garland Museum, the shoes' owner, and the insurance company. It's the first time everyone has been brought together like this and I'm hoping you'll help us out. I've got a few questions about Jared Canning and all indications are that you knew him best at the time of the crime. I'd really appreciate if you could give me a call back."*

He left his number twice and offered an alternate number, this one with a Chicago area code.

~~~~~

"Hi, Kelly, this is Detective Richards from the Grand Rapids Police Department. We spoke a few years ago regarding Jared Canning's involvement with the theft of the Ruby Slippers?"

Kelly walked around the edge of her desk and had one hand on the door when Ben walked by. Their eyes met and he moved like he was going to come into her office, but she pointed at the cell phone and quickly closed the door. She kept her back to the lab door as she kicked it shut to avoid whoever might be in there.

"Yes, I remember you."

"I'm calling because, as you may have heard, we have a new investigator working on the case."

She shook her head. She shouldn't have answered the phone, but she was busy and hadn't looked at the caller ID. Stupid.

"Kelly? You there?"

"Yes. Yes, I heard. What can I do for you?" She'd built belief in her innocence by always cooperating. As long as she didn't act like she was hiding anything, they seemed to believe she was simply a grieving girlfriend who didn't know better than to let herself be charmed by a lying con man.

"Mark McDonald is the investigator's name. He's been trying to get in touch with you to ask some questions, and said he wasn't able to connect. I told him I'd give you a call."

Kelly took a deep breath. She needed to keep Detective Richards on her side, but she didn't want to submit to questioning, especially with a new person. "I'm really not comfortable talking about it. I've told the police everything I know. I know a lot of people think I know where the shoes are—I still get threats—but I've got to consider my daughter. I don't want to open myself up to any more speculation or harassment."

"This guy is legit, I assure you," Richards said. "But I completely understand your hesitation. Would you be willing to meet with him if I came along?"

She had to think about her answer. She'd always liked Richards; even before she'd been cleared of suspicion he'd been respectful of her, which is more than she could say for some of the other cops. There was the one that got in her face and yelled at her, told her he was going to implicate her parents and send them to jail if she didn't tell him where the shoes were; several looked like they wanted to rip her clothes off every time she walked in; one asked if she knew what happened when you had a baby in prison. "I'm not being interrogated again."

"I understand. How about coffee? Let him ask you a few questions, cross it off his list?"

She weighed her options.

"I'll be there," Richards assured her.

"Okay."

"Great. You still in the area?"

"No, I'm in Duluth. But I'll be in Rapids this weekend."

"Sounds good. I'll set something up and call you with the details."

She hung up and sank into her seat. Should she call her lawyer? She hadn't talked to him in years, and he'd never been much help anyway. But he'd also never asked about her guilt or innocence and insisted he didn't want any details unless she was arrested. He told her to cooperate as much as possible without implicating herself, and it must have worked, because eventually the cops left her alone.

There was a growing knot in her stomach. No matter how much she tried, she couldn't ignore the fact that the shoes were in her trunk. She was afraid of the outright lie she'd have to tell, but it was more than that. She'd tried to research him, but there was no information about McDonald online. Just a page with the firm logo and phone number. None of the news outlets had his picture, and his name was too generic to look up on any social media. There was something about him that worried her but she wasn't sure what it was.

~~~~~

At three, Kelly sent a quick IM to Mira, Joel and Ben saying she needed to leave early but would be working from home later. She didn't wait for a response, just packed up, got in the car and drove toward the lake. In Canal Park she got a coffee and took it down to the lake walk. Waves crashed relentlessly against the rocks and there were little kids, pants rolled up around their knees, splashing in the cold water. Adults sat on lawn chairs and lay on blankets wearing the full range of clothes: pants and jackets to protect against the wind, t-shirts and shorts, all the way down to two-piece bikinis, soaking up the early summer sun. Seventy degrees was warm enough to tan after the endless winter they'd had. Even in her work clothes, Kelly wasn't out of place. There were several other people along the path in blouses and pressed pants, on break from their jobs downtown.

She walked out to the lighthouse and saw a boat in the distance, moving slowly toward the shore. In an hour or so the lift bridge would raise to allow it to pass.

Usually the waves, boats and sunshine calmed her. Today, the kids' screams pierced her ears and the loud, persistent whitecaps seemed to be warning her not to get too close.

She pulled out her phone to check the time. When she swiped her finger across the screen, her phone book opened and there, at the bottom, was a tiny picture next to the name Eric Stevens.

McDonald would have contacted him too.

She wanted to call him, talk through it like they talked through problems in high school. But what could she say? They'd never discussed anything about that summer: the shoes, the fact that they'd let their flirting go too far… At the beginning, while Eric was recovering, Kelly had thought about trying. But then the hallucinations started.

The last time she'd talked to him at all was the day of the press conference at Grace. She'd dropped the lunchbox off on his parents' porch when they weren't home and never checked to see if he'd gotten it.

Detective Richards set up the meeting with Mark McDonald for Sunday at ten a.m. The time worked well because Jordana enjoyed going to church with her grandparents, and they'd long ago stopped trying to talk Kelly into coming with them. She decided not to call Eric; if he'd been contacted and wanted to talk, he could call her. He wouldn't be able to help her, anyway, and she didn't want to add to his stress.

When they arrived in Grand Rapids on Saturday morning, Kelly's parents were outside: Susan working in her flower beds and John getting the boat ready. Kelly had barely stopped the car before Jordana was out, and when Kelly opened her door Jordana was there to tell her Grandpa was taking them all out on the lake.

An hour later, the four of them, along with Jordana's friend Erin, were in the middle of Pokegama

Lake. John had thrown the anchor and the girls were having fun diving off the bow, swimming for a few minutes, climbing in the back by the motor, and sprinting to the front to repeat.

They were wearing life jackets, and had both Susan and John watching them. Kelly leaned back and propped her feet on the side of the boat, a book in her lap. Soon her eyes were closed. The rocking of the boat, the rhythm of the girls' feet on the deck, and the heat lulled her into a trance. She wasn't quite asleep— she could hear the girls splashing and hear her parents' conversation— but dream-like images flashed through her mind.

She was inside Grace, in Eric's tunnel. There was blood on her hands. The Ruby Slippers were on the floor next to her, blood dripping off the heels. Then she was in the barn at Whiteside, trying to get out. Eric's body, a bullet hole above his eye, was blocking the door. She tried to move him, but as soon as she touched him he turned into Brad, and his dead body flopped against her legs, blood soaking through her jeans.

She jolted awake. The book flew out of her hands and landed with a small splash in the lake.

"Oh, crap, Mom, I'm sorry," Jordana said. She used the fishing net to recover the book and tried to dry it with her sopping-wet towel.

It took Kelly a moment to orient herself, to remember where she was, that she and Eric were both safe. The shoes were locked in the trunk of her car. Her legs were wet, with water Jordana had dripped over them, trying to wake her up.

Erin sat on the bow of the boat, wrapped in a towel, teeth chattering. Jordana sat next to her. Kelly could tell they were both worried she was mad. "Water a little cold?" she asked.

Jordana smiled, obviously relieved. "It's only cold when you get out!" She held out her hand, Erin let the towel fall, and the girls ran to the edge and jumped. Their long hair hung in mid-air until their feet hit the water and pulled their bodies down. A split second later, the lifejackets popped them back up. While they laughed and splashed, Kelly found a semi-dry towel and worked on the book. The pages would curl a little, but it would be readable.

"You okay?" John asked.

She was glad he couldn't see her eyes behind her sunglasses. "Yeah. Why?"

"You've been really quiet," Susan said.

Kelly nodded. "Sorry. I'm tired. Work's been really busy. This is relaxing."

"Jordana doing okay?" John asked.

Kelly watched the girls playing for a minute before answering. Jordana seemed happy in Duluth, but she was always happier here. It made Kelly question her decision to move. "She's great. Still misses it here, though."

"We miss having you here," Susan said.

"But it's good for you to be out on your own," John added. "We're proud of how well you're doing."

It was good having her own space. She and Jordana had learned to depend on each other. But, especially now, Kelly missed the safety she felt with her parents.

~~~~~

When Kelly arrived at the restaurant, Detective Richards was already sitting at a corner booth with a steaming cup of coffee in front of him. He stood and extended his hand as she approached. "Hi there. I hear you're a big shot over in the mines now."

She smiled and shook his hand. "Thanks."

Back when the theft actually happened, Richards had been fresh out of training with his college football physique. Now, he still had the broad shoulders, but his once-tapered waist was round and pressed against the buttons of his uniform shirt. His duty belt looked uncomfortable when he was standing, and when he sat he had to wiggle a little to keep the gun and flashlight from pressing into the bottom of his stomach. His hairline had receded almost to the crown of his shaved head. The years hadn't been kind to him, and Kelly couldn't help but wonder how much of it was due to the stress of this case. Police incompetence was often cited as the reason the shoes were still missing.

"You've been promoted since the last time I saw you," she said.

He nodded. "Yeah, a few years ago. Overall, it's about the same, but the hours are a little better."

She smiled. "Congratulations."

"You want to get some coffee? McDonald should be here soon, but you can go order if you want."

"I haven't eaten yet. Is it okay if I get breakfast?"

Richards nodded and Kelly went to the counter. If she had to have this meeting, she might as well get some good food too, and this place had amazing omelets. She returned to the table a moment later with a laminated "23" on a metal stick in one hand and a latte in the other.

Richards put his phone down and looked up at her. "All set?"

She nodded and slid in across from him. "Can you tell me anything about this guy?"

"There's not much to tell. An enthusiast, I guess, but he's got the investigative experience. Ex-military or something. I wasn't too keen to bring him in, to be honest, but the chief okayed it so I couldn't argue."

Kelly nodded and sipped her drink. "Why now, though? Is there some new information?"

"Not that I know of." His eyes went up and over her head. She followed his gaze to a man with the physique of an actor or part-time body builder, in a polo shirt and athletic pants, crossing the restaurant toward them. Kelly could see the outline of his shoulders and pecs through the shirt, and couldn't help picturing the muscles on his slim waist.

When he smiled and offered his hand she felt the heat rise in her cheeks. Had he seen her looking?

"Hi, I'm Mark," he said and slid into the booth next to her. He reached across the table to shake Richards's hand. "Good to see you again."

They shook, then Richards had to adjust his belt again and Kelly felt sorry for him. Besides being physically uncomfortable, he had to work with a guy who looked like this?

"You going to get anything?" Richards asked.

McDonald shook his head. "Going to the gym after this. Can't eat before I work out."

The waitress arrived and set Kelly's omelet on the table without taking her eyes off McDonald. She looked to be about fifteen, and her whole neck and face turned red when McDonald smiled and thanked her. She tried to say something but stumbled over the words, and hurried away.

Kelly thought Mark's gaze lingered a little too low, a little too long, on the girl. And why was he sitting so close? She scooted herself against the wall. "Well, it might be rude to eat in front of you two, but I'm going to do it anyway." She cut a big bite from the omelet and shoveled it into her mouth.

McDonald smiled and Richards continued to look uncomfortable. They started talking about the weather, how great the weekend had been, and Kelly got worried. She didn't want to make friends with this guy, no matter how attractive he was. The less time they spent together the better. She certainly didn't want to hear about his workout routine or tell him anything about what she did in her free time. "Sorry," she interrupted as soon as her mouth wasn't completely full of food. "I've only got about thirty minutes, so if you don't mind, can we get started?"

"Of course," McDonald said. "I wanted to give you time to eat."

She shook her head. "I'm good. I'll chew between questions. What can I do for you?"

"First, I should probably introduce myself properly. I don't know what you've heard, so I'll give you the quick version. I'm based in Chicago. Been following this case for years, and my business is now in a position where I can take a break from the rest of the agency's work and devote myself to solving it. The police here have been kind enough to let me review all their old case files. I've also seen the insurance company's investigation, but I've decided to start over. Square one. I want to question everyone myself, get my own feel for the case."

He paused. Kelly thought he was probably waiting for her to reply, but she wasn't sure what to say. She wanted to ask what kind of authority he had, if she should contact her lawyer, but didn't want to seem defensive before he'd even started with the questions. She should have asked Richards about it before she'd agreed to the meeting, anyway. He wouldn't have been offended; he'd spoken with her lawyer nearly as often as he'd spoken to her.

"So," McDonald continued, "Richards has been kind enough to put us in touch. I understand why you didn't return my calls—I'm sure you've dealt with a lot of crazies over the years."

She nodded and took another bite of omelet as an excuse not to elaborate. She'd gotten threats on and off since the shoes were stolen, the complaints must have been in the case file. Some had been horrible. She didn't want to relive them.

"Don't worry. This will be completely painless." McDonald reached out and stroked her arm in what should have been a comforting gesture. Instead of the good tingles and electricity someone that looked like him should have left on her skin, all she felt was a weird heaviness. She shivered.

"Sorry, are you cold?"

She shook her head and looked at Richards. He'd pulled his phone out and wasn't showing any interest in their conversation. She wished he had chosen a table with chairs. She wanted space, and he looked like he could use some also.

"You were dating the thief?" McDonald asked.

"Alleged thief, you mean? Yes, I was dating Jared."

The smile on Mark's mouth didn't reach his steel-gray eyes. "I'm sorry. Yes. Alleged. I do understand there is a general consensus he took the shoes—"

"But he died before anything could be proven." She was being adversarial, but couldn't help herself. "So we say alleged. Because he still has a family."

"Yes, I'm sure he does," McDonald said. "Are you in touch with them?"

"I've never met his parents."

"Any other family?

Jordana's face flashed through her mind and Kelly crossed her arms as she shook her head. She was no longer hungry.

"Okay, then. What can you tell me about him?"

"What do you want to know?"

"Let's start with how you met."

There was no amazing story, they'd met at a bar, had a few drinks, and…

"Did you sleep with him the first night?"

Kelly shot a look at Richards, but he still wasn't paying attention. "I'm sorry, but what does this have to do with the shoes?"

McDonald smiled. This time, it did seem genuine. Even though his eyes stayed the same frosted-metal color. "I'm trying to get a better handle on Jared. The way I work," he patted her hand a few times, then let his hand rest on top of it, "is I try to get inside the head of the target. The better I know him, the more I can think like him, the better I can retrace his steps." He curled his fingers around Kelly's and squeezed gently.

She shivered again and pulled her hand away to take a long drink of coffee.

There was no indication he'd noticed her reaction. "How long were you together?"

"About four months. We met right after he moved here."

"Where did he move from?"

"Tennessee. Nashville area, I think."

McDonald nodded and it suddenly clicked for Kelly why this felt so disingenuous. He wasn't taking any notes.

Richards was still looking at his phone and Kelly realized he was playing a game.

Recording without permission was illegal. Wasn't it? But McDonald had to be documenting the interview somehow. Unless it wasn't really a legit interview.

"Kelly?"

He placed his hand on hers again. She recoiled, banged her elbow into the wall, and tried to cover by taking a bite of the omelet.

"Ouch! Funny bone! Sorry about that. You okay? You kind of spaced out, didn't you?"

The eggs were cold and rubbery in her mouth. She had to take a drink of coffee to swallow them. "I'm sorry. What were you saying?"

"It's okay. I'm sure this is hard for you. I was asking whether his family was still in Nashville."

Kelly shook her head. She had gone to the hospital to help the nurses find his parents' number in his phone, but only because the police had asked her to. She hadn't stuck around to see if they'd gotten through, but heard a few days later that he was cremated and the ashes shipped back to Tennessee for the funeral. She'd thought about trying to let them know about their granddaughter, but had no idea how they'd take it, or her. She didn't want to cause any more pain, and didn't need any more complications in her own life.

"I don't know," she said. "I really have never had any contact with them. Jared didn't talk to them when we were together."

McDonald nodded. "Can you tell me what it was like to be in a relationship with him?"

Kelly thought of how to answer. There was so much she could say, but she wanted to keep it short. The Jared she dated for the first few months was completely different than the Jared after the theft. "We were young," she finally said. "We fought a lot."

"Did he ever hit you?" Mark's eyes were shining now, like they should have been when he was smiling. His face was placid, but it looked like he was putting effort into not looking excited.

She squeezed her hands together to try to keep from shivering again. "Of course not. We didn't fight like that. We just argued."

"About what?"

She shrugged. "Everything. We were young. I was trying to prove to my parents that I was independent, and...I don't know what he was trying to prove. But it's pretty hard to have a good relationship when you're constantly trying to show that you don't need each other."

"Very true."

"We were young," Kelly said again.

"What do you know about the theft?"

"I know they think he did it. I know everything I read in the papers."

"Did he ever talk to you about it?"

"Actually stealing them?" It was a stall tactic. She couldn't contradict anything he might have read in the interviews from before, but she didn't remember what exactly she'd said back then. Her hand had stopped shaking so badly, and she took a drink of her coffee.

It had gotten cold. "We went to the museum together once, but that was because I wanted to go."

"I'm sure you must have blamed yourself." He reached out like he was going to hold her hand again, so she pulled it quickly back into her lap.

It was an odd thing to say, something only people who knew her really, really well, and knew the whole story, how much she had admired Judy Garland and loved the shoes, would presume. And he didn't seem to mind that she hadn't answered the original question. "I've never thought of it that way," she lied.

"Really? You introduced him to the shoes, the pride of your hometown, and then he stole them. You didn't blame yourself? Even after he died?"

"He died of a bone infection."

"That he got while trying to hide the shoes."

How was the broken bone possibly related? It didn't make any sense. Jared had hidden the shoes in his closet. Kelly still believed someone had broken in and taken them while he was in the hospital. But…she broke eye contact with McDonald and looked again at Richards. His eyes met hers briefly, then dropped back to the phone. Her stomach had turned to stone, but she took a bite of the cold omelet anyway, just to have a reason not to answer.

McDonald waited, though.

"It sounds like you know more about this than I do," she finally said.

He nodded. "Like I said: I've reviewed all the files."

She checked the time. "I've got to get going."

Richards put his phone down as if he had been waiting for a cue and scooted awkwardly to the edge of his bench. "Yeah, it's time for me to be getting back too."

She was so thankful she could have kissed him.

McDonald nodded and stood, but kept the bench blocked so she couldn't get out of the booth. "I do have more questions for you. You're in Duluth, right? Can we meet there sometime soon? I definitely don't want to inconvenience you in any way."

"I don't mind coming over," she said. "My family is here, and Jordana has friends here." As soon as the words were out of her mouth she regretted them. If he hadn't already figured out she had a daughter, he would have been able to do it on his own, but she didn't want to give him any reason to ask about her. She didn't want him anywhere near her.

He opened his mouth but she slid over and forced him to step back by standing. "It was nice to meet you. Good luck with your investigation." To Richards she said, "Thanks for setting this up. Have a nice day." They all shook hands and she walked out as quickly as she could without running.

Her family wasn't home from church yet, and she locked the door behind her when she got inside. She pulled up his number in her phone and pressed the *call* button. "Eric," she said to the voicemail, "I need to talk to you."

~~~~~

Eric heard the phone ringing, but didn't want to talk to Matt, not when he was this hung over. The kid would be able to tell something was wrong, he'd ask why daddy was sick, and before long Sherrie would be all up his ass about drinking too much.

Maybe he'd drink less if she let him see his son more. What difference did it make how much he drank? Even when he was completely sober he only got the kid a couple afternoons a month.

He stumbled to the bathroom and took a quick shower. In the kitchen he made himself two eggs in the microwave, dumped a bunch of salsa on top, and washed it all down with a beer. The best hangover cure was pure protein, spice, and alcohol. It'd worked for him since high school.

After he was done eating he finally checked the phone, and was a little excited to see the message was from Kelly. He hadn't meant to be a jerk the last time they talked. But he waited so long to call and say he was sorry that, by the time he was ready, it was too late. She understood, though— what he'd been through— what her being inside the mine and finding the lunchbox had brought back. She'd always understood him. Better than his parents, better than Sherrie even. Sherrie had never been in the mine with him, she didn't understand how safe he'd always felt there. Or how waking up in a cold, dark mine shaft was like waking up in your own grave. Kelly understood that. Even if they never talked about it.

He played the message twice, listening to her voice, trying to determine if the shaking, desperate quality of it was real or just his shitty cell phone. He couldn't fuck it up with her again, and decided not to call back until he'd planned exactly what he would say. Instead, he grabbed another beer, sat down on the couch and started flipping through TV channels. Fishing, hunting, church, infomercials... finally settling on a reality show where kids were doing stupid shit for...he couldn't tell what the payoff was. Skateboards and bowling balls were hitting guys in the crotch, bikes were sliding down rails and crashing. The whole thing was hilarious.

It was nearly two o'clock before he noticed he hadn't heard from Matt yet. He called Sherrie, but the phone went to voicemail. He called back twice, same thing, and then called her parents.

"Hi, Eric." Sherrie's mom, Melissa, answered the phone with the kind of sigh he was used to hearing from most adults he'd known since high school or college. It was supposed to say *We really care about you and wish you'd get your life together* but he knew it really meant *You're not good enough for us.* "Sherrie and Matt are out on the boat with Glen. I'll have her call you later."

Instead of a call, that evening Eric received a text-message picture of his son holding two sunfish by the gills in front of a glitter-blue lake. He made it his phone's background image and got himself another beer.

Matt called Monday morning and told him all about fishing. "Grandpa made us get up before the sun and we stayed on the lake all day. I'm really sorry, I wanted to call you, but Grandpa said no phones in the boat."

Eric rubbed the stubble on his face and tried to wake up. "It's okay, buddy, I understand. The fish looked amazing in the picture Mom sent."

"They were! We ate them for dinner. I got to scale them and everything."

"Everything? Did you fillet them too?"

Matt laughed. "No, Grandpa did that. The knife is too sharp."

"That's right. It is. Have a good day, buddy."

"Bye, Dad. Love you!"

Eric said "Love you too," but the line was already disconnected.

He sat on the edge of the bed in his boxers, sent a quick message to the office receptionist saying he'd be in late after an early meeting, and put the phone down on the dresser. In his top drawer, he found the little bag of pills right where he'd left it, folded into a pair of black socks with red stripes. He picked one out and swallowed it, waited five minutes, and when he didn't feel anything, took a second.

He remembered Kelly while he was eating breakfast. By then, he was also feeling the happy effects of the pills.

~~~~~

Monday mornings at ReEarth always started with full staff meetings, after which Kelly's team gathered in the lab for a departmental meeting. Many of the interns worked variable hours, so one of the agenda items was always reviewing the weekly calendar and everyone's schedules before discussing ongoing projects and new assignments. They were in the middle of reviewing the permitting issues for Whiteside, and discussing which parts of their research could continue when her phone rang. She glanced down as she silenced it and saw *Eric.* Her heart jumped into her throat. She had a strict no-phones-in-meetings policy, unless it was an emergency. The only reason she allowed cells in meetings at all was because she and Mira had to be available for their children. The interns, and Joel for that matter, all left their phones at their desks.

She debated the explanation she'd have to make up if she answered the call and decided the lie was necessary. "Excuse me," she said.

She pushed the button to accept the call as she was walking out of the lab, but didn't speak until she'd closed the door to her office.

"Hey, there," Eric said.

"Eric." The room wasn't secure enough. Her whole team might hear everything she said. "Hang on a minute. I've got to…"

"Kelly. I've missed you."

His words were thick, but she couldn't tell if it was chemical or if he'd just woken up. When she got outside she said, "Just a second," and tried to avoid eye contact with the people walking in and out of the building, either just coming in (why were they so late?) or on their way to work sites and other meetings. Inside her car it was too stuffy with the windows rolled up, but at least private. "Sorry. Thanks for calling me back."

"Of course I called you back."

"Where are you?"

"Home. Summer cold.

She sucked air in through her teeth. He was high, and for some reason that made her hands itch for a cigarette. Even though she'd quit when Jordana was five, something about Eric brought everything back, made her feel like a teenager again. But she wasn't a kid. She *had* a kid. So did he. Even if he didn't feel the need to act like an adult, they needed to talk. "They're reopening the case. This guy out of Chicago. I had breakfast with him and Detective Richards yesterday morning." She shook her head. "What am I saying? They called you already, right? They said they're re-interviewing everyone."

"No."

"What?" His voice was so gravelly. She must have misunderstood.

"They haven't called me."

She heard the sound of cardboard sliding, something being tapped on the table. The mom in her, and pure jealousy, asked, "Are you smoking?"

"Just a cigarette."

"Put it out."

He laughed. "What?"

"I thought you stopped. You have a kid. You know how bad it is—"

"Wow. Hypocrite, anyone?"

"I quit when Jordana was in kindergarten," she said.

"Bullshit. I heard you. You're smoking right now."

The absurdity of it made Kelly laugh too. She was sitting still in a closed vehicle; there was nothing that could be confused for the sound of smoking, other than actual breathing. "I swear I'm not. But I wish I was."

"There. You can be good and live vicariously through me."

She laughed again.

"We should get together soon. When are you back in town?" he asked.

"How are you doing?" She rubbed the sweat out of her eyes.

"I'm good."

"Still at the landscape company?"

"Of course. It's mine."

"How are your parents?"

"Good. Went to Italy last winter. Can you imagine? My folks in Italy?"

She faked a laugh for him. "What are they doing this summer?"

"The usual. Dad's retired, but he's still at the office every day, so Mom's working in her garden and, I don't know...reading or something."

Kelly opened the car door to get some air, and dropped her voice. "Are you sure they haven't tried to get a hold of you at all? This guy seems pretty zealous. He called me at work."

"It's not hard to find where you work. You're all over the news." She heard him take a drag.

He was right. Nearly every night there was a clip of her saying something about the new mine or defending ReEarth—both their methods and intentions—played opposite a clip of hippie protesters foretelling the end of everything to love about Minnesota. It had been exciting, but now she wondered if she should be worried.

"It's the only reason I watch."

She left his comment hanging for a moment, not sure how to respond. Finally, she said, "I've got to go. But you'll let me know if you talk to McDonald? Or Richards?"

They didn't need to compare stories and she wasn't worried about him implicating her, but there was still something about McDonald that didn't sit well. She had been hoping Eric's perspective would help. But as he started rambling about how hard it was to run a company and take care of a child, she realized he wouldn't be looking at this with the eyes of someone with years of life between now and the stupid things they'd done as teenagers. He was still acting like a kid himself.

"I'm sorry," she said, interrupting him. "I've got to get back to work."

"Sure thing," he said. "Let me know next time you're in Rapids. We should get a drink."

She made a noise, neither agreeing nor declining, and hung up.

~~~~~

By the time she got back to the office, the meeting was over and everyone was back at their own desks. Ben was standing by the coffee pot and he turned, wearing the same expression as he'd had when she took the call from Richards last week, then followed her into her office.

She tried to come up with an acceptable explanation in her head as he closed the door and leaned against it. This was serious. Could he possibly know what was going on? Or was she being fired? Bad things came in threes, right?

"Are you okay?" he asked.

"I'm fine." She perched on the side of her desk, and tried not to seem at all worried about why he was there.

"You've seemed...I don't know. Worried, I guess. I wanted to make sure." He crossed the distance between them and stood a little too close. They'd dated secretly for almost six months. When it started to get serious she broke it off. Neither of them wanted to look for a different job, and she had enough problems asserting her authority—being in a relationship with the boss wouldn't help at all. But she still missed him, and had to fight the urge to rest her head against his chest.

He made it harder by putting his hands on her shoulders and locking her with his brown eyes. "I'm here. If you need anything."

Her stomach leapt to her throat. He let his hands drop. But he didn't drop her gaze, and she had to look away. She could still feel the heat from each of his fingers, gentle but strong.

~~~~~

Kelly felt simultaneously behind at work and guilty about the hours she was putting in. Jordana was often the first child dropped off at her summer program and one of the last picked up, Kelly brought work home with her almost every night, although she did make an effort not to start on it until Jordana was in bed. The permitting regulations for the mines seemed to change weekly, sometimes daily, and it was all she could do to keep ahead of it. And the protesters.

Minnesotans for Minerals was organizing regular demonstrations, claiming the underground mines were dangerous, citing the collapse of the coal mines in West Virginia and Turkey as proof no one should be underground. Plus, they said, the methods used to extract the minerals from the rock would release toxic chemicals into the underground water supply with the potential to contaminate Lake Superior, the Boundary Waters, and even the Mississippi River. They wanted operations at Grace closed immediately, and an injunction against all future underground mining.

Most of it was conjecture, and some of it was downright ridiculous, but it was easier to believe "tree huggers" than a "huge, profit-hungry corporation." No one seemed to care that ReEarth was owned and staffed mostly by people from the area, and they were as dedicated to making sure the mines would be safe for the workers and the environment as anyone with a bird or tree on their logo.

Jordana went to a sleepover and Kelly spent the weekend holed up in her office, periodically hitting *ignore* on her phone when Eric's name popped up. It was as if he'd taken her phone call as an invitation to start pursuing her again. She cared about him as a friend. That was it. There would be nothing romantic, and she wouldn't go out with him. He didn't seem to get it, though. She checked the messages only because she wanted to know if he had been contacted by the new PI, and grew increasingly concerned each time he said he hadn't.

*K*elly, *I know you're grown up and important now, but I also know you helped Jared. You know where he hid the shoes. You are as responsible as he was, and you're still alive. That means you're going to help find them, and then you're going to jail.*

As soon as she hit the delete button, Kelly wished she could get the message back. She was angry. It was harassment and she should have called the cops. But now she had no proof. It had been years since someone had threatened her in hopes of getting a confession. She was out of practice.

She didn't recognize the number. An internet search told her it was a Montana area code, but that was it. Her hands were shaking as she rechecked the locks on the apartment door and wished she had installed her own deadbolt, one that no one, including the building owner, had a key for. There was nothing she could do tonight, though. She took her blanket and pillow into Jordana's room and locked that door too.

As she lay there, listening to Jordana breathing, the sounds of doors opening and closing all over the building seemed amplified. It was never very loud, and most of what she heard was quiet laughing and shushing, people trying to be polite even though they were intoxicated. Every time she heard a man's voice she held her breath until she was sure it didn't match the one from the message. Other than Mrs. McAlester she didn't know many of her neighbors. The building was mostly college students and older people. There were a few young couples on other floors, but Jordana seemed to be the only child.

After dismissing the idea that the message might have been from McDonald, disguising his voice, Kelly thought about calling and asking him for advice. There was something about him that absolutely terrified her. At the same time, she was incredibly attracted to him. He could protect her. But it was an old habit, pursuing the dangerous relationship. It was how she'd ended up with Jared. He was from out of town, attractive, and didn't care about anyone or anything in Grand Rapids. Except, of course, the shoes. But she didn't know that until it was too late.

~~~~~

At some point she fell asleep and ended up with her head pressed against Jordana's nightstand. In the morning she had a sore back and a stiff neck, but also the beginning of a plan.

"What are you doing?" Jordana sat up and rubbed her eyes while Kelly was trying to silently gather her bedding and sneak out.

"Shhh. It's too early to get up. Go back to sleep."

"Why are you in here?"

"I was just checking on you."

"Why do you have all that stuff?"

Kelly looked at the pile in her arms as if she didn't know it was there. "Maybe I was sleepwalking." She bent over and kissed Jordana's forehead, then went out the door.

It *was* too early to be up, but she wasn't going back to sleep, so she started a pot of coffee and took a shower. Her resolve solidified as the hot water helped loosen the knots in her body.

She would return the shoes this week. The whole backpack would be left in a box at the Grand Rapids mall, in the center atrium where the picnic tables were. She'd put the museum's address and correct postage on it so whoever found it could give it to the mailman when he came. The mall was old and partially empty. There was no reason it would have security cameras.

Once they were back at the museum, the harassment would stop. Mark McDonald would go back to Chicago. Everyone knew Jared had taken them, and he was dead. There would be no reason to spend the time and money trying to figure out where they'd been.

~~~~~

"Hey, Barry, how's it going?" Eric asked as he knocked on the doorframe.

The name had always cracked him up. It sounded like the name of an accountant or a lawyer, and Barry was both. He was in his mid-sixties with a pot belly and a bald spot he tried to cover with the single wisp of black hair growing out of the crown of his head. Every morning he combed it meticulously to the left with gel, but by ten those few hairs had staged a revolt, sticking out at random angles and leaving his shining scalp bare. Even worse was the way Barry sweated as the day went on. By mid-afternoon the hair looked like weeds flattened by a river current. There were several theories about why he didn't cut it off, but, based on the motorcycle he drove and the leather jacket he wore, most everyone thought he was trying to hold on to his youth. And trying to be cooler than any lawyer/ accountant ever could be.

Barry had been one of Stevens' Landscaping's first employees and, other than Eric's dad, Dale Stevens himself, had stuck around the longest. He was a hard worker, made great eggnog at Christmas, and was in charge of distributing paychecks. Everyone loved him.

"I'm good! Good to see you." Barry stood to give Eric a hug. His wooden desk had three file folders labeled Accounts Payable, Accounts Receivable, and To Be Filed; a "World's Greatest Grandpa" coffee mug; and an old ten-key calculator. The computer keyboard and monitor seemed like an afterthought, especially when Barry sat down and Eric saw how he would need to turn in his chair to type anything. "You haven't been around lately," Barry said, although not accusingly. "We've missed you."

Eric leaned on the edge of a low bookcase in the corner and nodded. "Been working on some stuff. We should be getting some new clients shortly." The lie was getting old, even to Eric's ears, but it seemed whenever he said it, someone inevitably called and booked their services. He was fine with taking credit even when it had nothing to do with him or the imaginary meetings he kept telling people he was having. He pretended to notice the newspaper sitting on the top of the bookcase, a big picture of the ruby slippers on the front, and picked it up. "What do you think of this?" He'd overheard Barry giving legal opinions on the work of the new private investigator in the break room and had questions he didn't want to ask in front of the other employees, so he'd come in early and planted the paper next to Barry's family photos. "Crazy they still haven't found anything, right?"

"It's a damn shame is what it is. The young man that took those shoes... by God if he wouldn't have died on his own—"

"Whoa, whoa," Eric said, holding up his hands. "You know Jared was a friend of mine, right?"

When Barry frowned his thick eyebrows merged above his nose. "I do know, and it's a good thing you got your act together. I can't believe you ran around with people like him. You're better than that."

Eric looked at his shoes. He hadn't anticipated the scolding and forgot what he was there to say.

"And the other thing," Barry continued, "this PI. I know they say he's volunteering his time, but there's no way this isn't costing taxpayer money in terms of police time. For what? If the shoes are around, I highly doubt they've been taken care of. They're probably trash. And it's not like they could charge anyone with the crime. We all know that southern boy did it. He's dead. Even if he had help, the statute of limitations is up."

Bingo. That's what Eric had heard him say in the break room. "What do you mean?"

"The statute of limitations! You can't charge anyone for a theft after seven years in Minnesota. It's over. Move on, people. The shoes are gone." Barry grabbed the newspaper and threw it into his trash. "I'm sorry. You came in here for something and I've been rattling on."

"No, it's fine. I really just came to say 'Hi.'"

"That was nice of you, son. Do it again soon, okay?"

Eric smiled and nodded as he left. He told the receptionist he was going out and dialed Kelly on the way to the car.

~~~~~

"Hey, Kelly, I need to talk to you. Call me back as soon as you can."

Kelly played Eric's voicemail three times, listening to his voice. It was clear and confident. Adult. No slurring. Urgent, but not desperate. Maybe he'd finally talked to McDonald. She hit the button to call him back.

She could hear the smile in his voice when he answered. "You don't have to worry about that investigator."

She hated it when people didn't say "Hello" when they answered the phone. "What?"

It sounded like his fingers were tapping on something, keeping time with a classic rock song blaring from his radio. "You don't have to worry about the investigation."

She rubbed her forehead. There wasn't enough coffee in the world to help her decipher what Eric meant, especially this early in the morning. "Can you turn your radio down? What are you talking about?"

The radio got quieter. "Statute of limitations. They can't charge anyone with the theft anymore."

Immediately she wondered if the call was being monitored. Whether it was a setup to try to get her to admit being involved. Maybe that's why he wasn't talking to McDonald, maybe he'd made some sort of deal giving him immunity if he could implicate her. But she wasn't involved in the actual theft. And there was no way he could know she had the shoes now. No one did. She chose her words carefully and tried to keep her tone flat. "That's interesting. How do you know?"

"I asked our company lawyer."

She forced herself to swallow the hot coffee in her mouth and not spit it all over the dash. "You what?"

"Yeah. I asked him what he thought of the case. He told me it was a waste of time and money because the statute of limitations had run out."

What, exactly, was said between Eric and the lawyer? Was it still Barry? She wanted to know what he'd *thought,* beyond what he might have said. And what if Eric hadn't asked the right questions, or had misunderstood his analysis? He'd never been worried about being connected to the theft. He'd been questioned only because he knew Jared; no one ever thought he'd had anything to do with it. That accusation they'd saved for her alone. She was publicly tried and convicted without ever being arrested. And now, after all the work she'd done to prove everyone wrong, the shoes were in her car, proving them right.

"Kelly?" Eric's voice broke through her thoughts.

"Yeah, sorry."

"I thought I lost you."

"No, I'm here."

"That's all I called for."

Now he was mad. Talking to him was worse than talking to a child.

"They can't be trying to connect you to the theft because it wouldn't do any good. It wouldn't matter. They're just trying to find the shoes."

When the phone rang for the third time that afternoon she answered and pretended not to know about the other calls. "Hi, Mark."

"Kelly! Hi! I've been trying to get a hold of you."

"Really? I'm sorry, I've been in meetings all day. I haven't had my phone on me."

"I still have those questions for you. I'll be in Duluth this afternoon. Could I come by your office?"

"I don't think that would be a good idea." More than anything, she didn't want him here where people would see him and ask more questions, or connect him to the constant ringing of her cell phone.

"I need to speak with you today," he said.

"We're speaking now." There was a purposeful amount of sarcasm in her voice. "And I made myself available for our meeting a few weeks ago. I have work to do and a family to think about."

"Yes, I know. You are currently working on reopening old iron ore mines for their possible copper and nickel reserves, but you're running into problems with your permits. In fact, just last week you had to suspend nearly all work at your first location, Grace. The mine is just outside of Chisholm, and one of the places we think Jared may have hidden the Ruby Slippers."

"What—"

"Whiteside is sitting there, waiting," McDonald continued as if he hadn't just given a completely new theory of where the shoes might have been and Kelly hadn't spoken at all. "Your parents, Susan and John, live in Grand Rapids. Your daughter, Jordana, is in a summer program at the rec center in Hermantown from around six thirty in the morning until you pick her up around six each night."

Kelly's stomach sank down to her knees, but her lunch came up and sat in the back of her throat. "How do you know all that?"

"I do my research," he said. "If I could find the information I need without asking you, I would. I need to know more about Jared, and you're the only one who can help me. I can always ask your parents what they know about the theft. Or maybe see if Jordana knows who her dad is?"

"I'll meet you at the coffee shop in Canal Park at three."

"See you there."

She sat in her chair, shaking, until Ben poked his head through her door. It had been open the whole time.

"You look awful," he said.

"I'm not feeling very well." She tried to compose herself. "I'm going to get some air."

"Do you want some company?"

Yes. Please come with me. More than anything she didn't want to go alone, but it was the only option.

~~~~~

McDonald had picked one of the small two-person tables in the corner near windows, wedged between the fireplace and bathrooms, as far from the counter and the door as possible. There were only a few other people in the coffee shop; most were taking their drinks down by the lake. She'd been hoping to beat him there and snag a place right in the front where everyone coming and going would pass them.

"Did you want anything?" he asked as she approached the table.

She shook her head. "I had to promise to bring stuff back for everyone, so I'll grab it on my way back to the office. I've got twenty-five minutes."

He smiled. "You sound like a great boss."

The compliment caught her off guard, as did the smile.

"First of all, I want to apologize. I understand from Detective Richards I may have intimidated you with all of the phone calls. The way I was dressed when we first met wasn't very professional, either. I didn't mean to come off as a hit-man." He chuckled. "And on the phone a little while ago—I realize I may have sounded threatening."

She didn't notice she'd been holding her breath until she felt her lungs deflate. Today his eyes had a blue-green tint and sparkled like maybe he was actually happy. His creamy bronze tan was obviously natural, the result of spending a lot of time outside. Even his muscles didn't look oversized or scary. Everything about him looked friendly, from his blue-striped button-down shirt and jeans to the brown glasses he hadn't worn at the last meeting.

"I'm very passionate about this case, and I've done a ton of research into everyone involved, no matter how peripherally. I forget sometimes what my physical presence, and my persistence, can say to people." He flashed that smile again, maintaining eye contact as he took a long drink of water. "And, earlier, I was trying to convey that I'm not going to waste your time. If this information was something I could find on my own, I would have. I realize it may have seemed threatening. I'm working on it."

She felt heat rising in her cheeks and had to look away. He was no longer an attractive bad boy, he was gorgeous and *nice.* "Apology accepted. What can I do for you?"

"My goal is simply to find the shoes. I'm not a cop. I can't charge anyone with anything. It wouldn't matter, anyway. The statute of limitations has run out. Whoever was involved is going to get off scot-free, but the shoes are still out there somewhere. They're an American treasure and I want to return them."

Kelly laughed. "American treasure? You really are passionate about these shoes."

He nodded. "I am."

"Just out of curiosity, who are you returning them to? Who hired you?"

"No one hired me. I'm doing this on my own. And I don't know who will get them. I'll turn them over to the police, but the owner received an insurance settlement already, so he'd have to pay that back in order to take possession. Maybe the insurance company, if they want to deal with selling them."

"What about the museum?"

"They were never the museum's property."

It was one of the facts everyone had known but always seemed to forget. Maybe she should reconsider who to address the box to when she left it at the mall. Maybe the museum was the wrong place to send them. But part of the plan had been for the box to be opened and the bag and shoes handled enough to cast doubt on using *any* fingerprints they might find. She blinked and nodded, turning her attention back to the conversation. "How can I help you?"

"You were closest to Jared. Like I said before, I'm looking for any information as to where he might have hidden the shoes. Where he went in the days between stealing them and when he died. Specifically the weekend between when he broke his ankle and went to the hospital. Who'd he hang out with? The other guy who was killed around the same time—Brad something—did you know him?"

Kelly nodded.

"I think he might have been involved. Did the two of them get along? Were they together a lot?"

The questions about Brad threw Kelly off. She'd never considered a connection between him and the shoes. "I didn't know Brad that well," she finally said. "I was friends with his cousin—"

"Eric?"

It was disconcerting that McDonald knew everyone's name. Then he smiled, as if he could sense her unease, and said, "Remember? I'm an investigator. I do my research."

She tried to smile, but her lips wouldn't move. Why wasn't he questioning Eric? Everything within her was conflicted. She was afraid of this man, but also attracted to him. Her mind was telling her to run, but her body was rooted to the seat, willing to move only if it was to get closer to him.

"Brad and Jared didn't like each other," she said. "I don't know if they went anywhere together, ever. Sometimes they were in the same place, like at the bar or whatever, and Brad was in Jared's apartment a few times..." her voice drifted off. The only time she knew about Brad ever being at Jared's was the night she found the shoes.

Mark's eyes narrowed but the smile stayed on his lips. Like he was reading her thoughts, but trying to look friendly so she'd keep talking. She was horrified she had been attracted to him a moment before and shivered involuntarily.

"The last time I saw him at Jared's they almost got into a fight." She picked up her phone and checked the time. "I don't know if they ever talked again."

"What was the fight about?"

"Me. Brad said something about me, and Jared punched him." It was true enough. She could still remember Brad's slimy gaze on her legs and chest. How she'd felt naked in Jared's t-shirt. The Ruby Slippers, in Jared's backpack, lying at her feet. She shivered again.

"Are you cold? They have the air really high in here. Do you want to get a hot drink? Or go out in the sun?"

"Um, yeah." Kelly tried to regain her composure. "But I've got to get going, I have to get back to the office. Sorry I couldn't help you more."

"It's okay, I appreciate your time. I might call you again." As he stood, she noticed his cowboy boots and almost laughed. She was going to say something, but he reached out and grabbed her hand more gently than a man of his size should have been able to. Her stomach flipped over as her eyes met his and her body moved a few steps closer.

"Of course," she said.

~~~~~

Thanks for taking the time yesterday. Maybe after all this is over I could take you out for coffee and you could ask the questions. The bouquet was simple, a card shoved in the middle of some wildflowers tied with a bow.

Kelly smiled to herself. She needed to be careful, but Mark was...She tried not to think about how attractive he was. Or that she'd started thinking about him as "Mark" instead of "McDonald."

She was arranging the vase on the corner of her desk when Ben came in. There was a question in his eyes as he looked from the flowers to her, but he didn't ask it, just said, "We need to talk, right now."

The smile left her face.

"Get your team to the conference room. No interns."

She, Joel and Mira walked together into the same room where Kelly had first signed her ReEarth employment contract. The view was no less beautiful, but Ben had been right. She'd long ago gotten used to it. The lake was more or less just...there...like a painting she'd seen too many times to fully appreciate. Already seated was a new guy from legal—Kelly couldn't remember his name—and Frank with his trainee, Jim Stanton. When Daniel Kaur, the finance guy, came in with Ben, Kelly realized it was really serious. Nichole Karr, ReEarth's PR rep, was the last in. She looked frazzled—her normally sleek hair was a poofy mess and dark circles swelled under her eyes. She sat next to Ben, and Kelly noticed how bad he looked too: his shirt was wrinkled and his tie crooked, as if he'd gotten dressed in the dark and hadn't looked in a mirror since. He was wearing glasses for maybe the second time since Kelly had met him.

She felt a flash of jealousy. Were they disheveled because they'd been together? Things with her and Ben had been over for a long time, but still…

"It looks like Burdock is pulling his support." Ben said.

Oh. That's why Ben and Nicole hadn't gotten any sleep. Joel and Kelly's eyes met across the table. Mira raised one eyebrow and shook her head almost imperceptibly.

Ben explained that Minnesotans for Minerals had gotten ReEarth's favorite State Senator to change his position on underground mining in general. "This isn't just delays and additional environmental studies. This could be the end of operations. For both Grace and Whiteside. Everything we've been working for."

"We have the data on our side," Kelly said. "All of their objections—"

"They do too," Ben interrupted. "Their new studies show significant risk of contaminating the ground water with repercussions all over the United States." He rubbed a hand through his hair and slid a stack of papers across the table. "This is the preliminary report they're releasing tomorrow. We've got to get ahead of it somehow."

"But it's crazy," Kelly said, grabbing one of the stapled packets. "We've tested the water."

"It doesn't matter. They've pulled our permits. Grace is now closed."

"What?" Everyone at the table started talking at the same time, asking questions, flipping through the report.

Nicole held up her hand. "We're going to get working on infographics with the information we have refuting this for distribution both online and as a newspaper stuffer in the next few days. We can turn this around. Kelly, how soon can you give us new tests?"

Kelly was scanning the papers and said without looking up, "Hang on. I'm trying to figure out what I'm testing for."

Everyone started flipping through the packets of information, but Kelly, Joel and Mira all read the conclusion at the same time and looked up at each other, mouths open. "This is…" Kelly couldn't think of anything to say that wouldn't cost her job. If she told Ben the data was right, ReEarth was over. The amount of time it would take to retest and create new proof… "I can reiterate our current stance, at least while we work to validate this, but I can't get anything new for a few weeks," she said to Nicole. "Knowing that, how long do we have?"

Ben turned to Daniel and the guy from legal.

"We've got cash to get us two more months, right now," Daniel said. "But we're going to start losing funding fast."

"If this plays out," the legal guy added, "there will be legislation by the end of the year that will close our current operations."

Kelly nodded.

Nicole said, "But we've got some time. We can launch a campaign today. We'll highlight three things: job growth with the mines, our reclamation and environmental efforts, and the economic potential for the area. A side by side of the old, shuttered Grace mine—and maybe some of the shuttered downtown businesses from a dozen or so years ago—and the new mine and new growth will play well. We've got some stuff about half-ready, it was going to be for a feel good campaign closer to the holidays, but we can use it all now."

Kelly looked at Joel. "You're old friends with Burdock, right?"

Joel shrugged. "We haven't talked in a while."

"Take him golfing or fishing or whatever he wants to do," Ben said, pulling a credit card from his wallet and throwing it to Joel, Frisbee style. "Find out what is really swaying him. We all know this isn't about some made up theories about us draining Lake Superior."

"Wait—is that what they're saying?" Kelly let herself get a little excited. Their data said nothing about draining the lake. Seriously contaminating it, yes, but if they couldn't even read their own information…

"No," Ben said. "I wish it was." He ran his hands through his hair. "Go. We'll reconnect in a few hours if we have anything new." Everyone started to stand. "Kelly," he said. "Hang back a minute."

She nodded and flipped through the report while everyone filed out, starting to formulate a plan in her mind. When the door closed, she looked up. Ben was sitting in the chair Joel had been in, directly across from her, rubbing the stubble on his chin and neck.

"What do you think? Really?"

She decided direct honesty was the only option, even though it was going to hurt. "Just glancing at this…" she took a deep breath. "We've tested extensively. I don't believe what we're doing is harming the area. I wouldn't be on board if it was. However, what they've got is compelling. I need some time to look into it."

He nodded. "Do you have what you need?"

"I think so. I've got Joel and Mira."

"You can't let the interns know anything about this."

"What should I do?"

"Send them to work with Nicole for the next few days. They don't need to know why we're creating the marketing."

Kelly nodded and, instinctively, reached across the table and grabbed his hand. "It'll be okay." He closed his fingers around hers and they locked eyes for a split second too long.

Ben dropped her hand and pushed his chair away from the table. "I'll talk to you later."

He'd had to reschedule his afternoon with Matt. He hated to do it, but just thinking about meeting with Kelly—he was too nervous to pay attention to a child, especially his son, so full of endless energy.

He'd talked her into going to Applebee's because: one, it was close; and two, they had good happy hour specials. He smiled at himself in the mirror, thinking about how she'd been worried she would run into people she knew. It was cute. She was nervous. Everyone she'd worked with was long since grown up and gone off, just like she had.

It didn't bother him, still being in town. For one thing, more and more people were moving back as they had kids and decided they didn't want to raise them in the Cities or Duluth. Besides, he wasn't here because it didn't work out somewhere else, he'd moved back to run his company.

He finished shaving, rinsed the razor, splashed lukewarm water on his face and dressed in a dark-gray soft cotton polo shirt and jeans. While he was threading his belt, he solidified his resolve to tell her everything. Kelly must have been involved too, so if he laid it all out there, made her feel comfortable enough to be honest with him…It was a bond only the two of them shared. Only she could understand what it was really like to see the coverage in the papers every year. To know.

It was too early to leave, so he grabbed a beer out of the fridge and sat down in front of the golf tournament on TV. He didn't realize how thirsty he was, and quickly went back to the fridge for another. By the time he left, there were three empties on the table in front of him and a half-full bottle in his hand.

~~~~~

Kelly spotted Eric at a table in the back corner of the bar with a beer in front of him and let out a long sigh, hoping he wasn't already drunk. She didn't want to be here. The whole trip to Grand Rapids couldn't have come at a worse time, but she'd agreed to let Jordana spend the week with John and Susan. Her plan to leave the shoes in the mall wasn't solid enough to act on yet, she was still trying to figure out a way to possibly clean any fingerprints there might be off the sequins, so they were still in the trunk, which hadn't been opened since Kelly had hid them there. When Eric called and said he had very important news, she'd agreed to meet only because she was already in town.

"Hey," she said.

"I helped Jared." He took a long drink as she slid into the booth and removed her jacket.

"When he broke his leg? I know." If this was what he'd called her here for...

He shook his head, but the waitress showed up before he could continue.

Kelly ordered water with lemon and cringed when he ordered another beer. This was a waste of time. He was here to drink. The same man he'd always been—barely capable of responsibility. That was probably what pushed him and Jared together that summer. He'd probably already known Sherrie was pregnant and was afraid of losing his freedom.

"That's not what I mean," Eric said as soon as the waitress was out of earshot. "I mean...I *helped* him. With the...you know..." he waved his hands in a little circle over the table.

Kelly studied his glassy eyes and wished she knew how drunk he was. She wasn't sure whether to believe anything he was saying, or if she even cared to know the truth. What she wanted to say was "Shut up and leave me alone." What she actually said was, "Mark asked to have another meeting with me." Eric would have connected with him by now, and she wanted to know what their meeting had been like. It was really the only reason she was there.

"Again?"

"Yeah. We did another phone interview too." These conversations had gone much like the first two, lots of questions about Jared that Kelly tried to answer, some accusations, apology, flirting. It was like he really couldn't control his temper flares, but was able to quickly rein them in. Scary. And intriguing.

"So this will be—what? The third time you've talked to him?"

"Fourth. I met him in Duluth once too. What happened when you talked to him?"

Eric shrugged and polished off his beer as the waitress arrived with the fresh glass and Kelly's water. He smiled, thanked her, then turned back to Kelly. "Nothing. He hasn't called me."

"What?"

"He hasn't called me."

"But you… you were there. You came to see him the day he died. And…"

"I know." Eric raised his glass like he was toasting something, and winked. "And I was *involved.*"

"Then why…he said he's trying to recreate Jared's last few days by interviewing everyone who knew him. Why not talk to you?"

"No one has ever suspected I had anything to do with it. I had better connections than you. And I didn't freak out at the crime scene."

"Fuck you." The words were soft, but felt good. She was tired of being so put together all the time. Of course she'd freaked out when she found out Jared was dead. She was there to tell him she was carrying his child. Wanting to protect him was only natural. And it wasn't like it mattered. The shoes weren't there, and she didn't know where they were. When the cops found out she was pregnant, they justified her reaction for her. Hormones.

Eric raised his eyebrows and started to smile. "There's my Kelly," he said.

"No." She wasn't going to lose control of the situation. She took a deep breath. "Both Richards and Mark told me they were re-interviewing *everyone.* Mark said he'd read all the files, but he's starting from the beginning himself. It doesn't make any sense for them not to have contacted you. Are you sure—"

"You're right," Eric cut her off and signaled the waitress for two more beers. "It doesn't. Have you gone all the way through Grace yet?"

The change of subject caught her off guard. "Yeah, we were open for a little while, but had to close for now. Permitting issues."

Eric nodded but didn't speak.

"You need a job?" She didn't really want to stick her neck out for him, but something entry level, with union pay and benefits, might be good. Having an imposed schedule instead of being the boss...maybe he'd get himself together.

"No, I'm good there. That's where Jared hid them, though."

She was sure she'd misunderstood.

"What?"

"We put them in the mine."

"But then…" Mark had said the same thing. They were working together. Kelly wasn't sure if she should order a beer and try to calm down, or if she should get Jordana and get out of town.

~~~~~

Eric studied her eyes as he thought back to that summer, and the fall after. They'd almost been something, but she'd moved in with her parents right after Jared died and he'd been in the hospital. They never had the chance to really talk before he went back to school. When she found out Sherrie was pregnant, she'd called, said he'd be a great dad, but never said anything about the rest of it. The next time he saw her, the following spring, she was very pregnant. He figured the baby must be Jared's and considered telling her then, but he was engaged to Sherrie, really trying to make a family. Now that Sherrie was out of the picture…

He reached out and rested his hand on hers, his voice barely a whisper. "I helped him. We put them back there, with the lunchbox. It was the day Jared broke his ankle—he was trying to jump across the creek."

Kelly blinked, but didn't pull her hand away.

"Then it got infected because he insisted on walking on it, going all the way in with me. If I would have gotten him to the hospital sooner… It's my fault." he shook his head. "I think Brad moved them."

"You don't know that."

Was she saying Brad didn't move them? That she did? If Jared had told Kelly where the shoes were before he died and she was the one that moved them, then she was the real reason for Brad's death, and why he'd been shot…

"Eric?"

He shook his head. No. She wouldn't have done anything like that. They'd been, if not in love, at least close. If they cooperated with each other now, they could find the shoes. Be the heroes. Together.

~~~~~

Kelly didn't know what to say.

She wanted to ask what Eric meant about Brad, but couldn't. There were too many lies, she didn't want to try to keep track of anything else while she was talking to Mark. McDonald. His comments were still running through her mind. He did know more about Jared than she did.

The fact that he hadn't talked to Eric—it was like he was trying to set her up, keep her talking until she contradicted herself. She needed to get rid of the shoes so everyone would stop looking. "I'm sorry," she slid off the stool. "I've got to go."

She was a half dozen steps away from the table when Eric called, "When's the meeting?"

She turned around. "What meeting?"

"McDonald."

A few heads turned, and she quickly walked back to the table to give him the details.

"I'm going," he said. "I'll sit and pretend to read the paper. I want to hear what this guy has to say. I'm worried about you."

She let him pull her into a hug, a little too tight, too intimate for their old friendship. "I'm worried about you too," she said.

When his alarm beeped on Monday morning he forgot why it was set so early, rolled over, and shut it off. Before he fell back to sleep he remembered, rolled the other way and sat up. If nothing else, he could protect her if things went bad. And if it turned out she did know where the shoes were, he could help her like he'd helped Jared.

The same clothes he'd worn the day before were hanging over a chair near the bed, so he pulled them on and went to the dresser. In the sock drawer he selected a single pill and swallowed it on his way out the door.

After ordering a small coffee, black, he chose a table near the window with an abandoned newspaper, and began reading the sports page. He recognized Detective Richards immediately when he walked in, but didn't allow their eyes to meet. He and Richards had an okay relationship, but he didn't feel like talking to the cop unless he was required to.

He turned the page and reached for his coffee cup, then heard the voice. The man entered through the coffee shop's side door and was hidden behind a rack of mugs and coffee pots as he ordered, so Eric couldn't see him. But there was no doubt. Liquid scalded his trembling fingers, hot coffee spilling over the cup suspended half way between the table and his mouth. He quickly set it down and grabbed a napkin.

"Eric," Detective Richards was standing over him. "How are you? Long time no see!" Richards's hand was extended, Eric had no choice but to reach out and shake it. The cop took this as an offer to sit, and started talking about the previous week's baseball games.

Eric tried to concentrate, to make conversation, but he'd seen the man that went with the voice.

Charles had gotten a haircut and put on about sixty pounds of pure muscle. Sunglasses and a baseball cap obscured his face, but Eric saw the boots. It was him, and he was coming over. There was no way for Eric to escape.

"Hey, Brian," Charles said, shaking Richards's hand. "Sorry I'm late."

"It's okay," Richards said. "I don't think Kelly's here yet anyway." He turned to Eric. "Eric, this is Mark McDonald, the PI working on the slippers case. Mark, this is Eric. We've talked about him a little bit—he was friends with Jared too."

McDonald took off his sunglasses.

Eric felt bile rising in his stomach. There was no doubt at all. McDonald was Charles. Charles was back. Charles was the one looking for the shoes. The one stalking Kelly.

Charles held out his hand for Eric to shake. "Nice to meet you."

Eric swallowed hard and left the hand hanging in the air long enough that Richards looked at him. "You okay?"

Eric blinked and looked at Richards, then back to Charles. He reached out and accepted the hand. "Yeah, sorry. Spaced out for a second. Nice to meet you too." He felt the color draining from his face. Charles's smile grew as he pumped Eric's hand, squeezing way too hard.

While Richards filled Eric in on the case, Charles pulled the chair next to him out and away, nearly to the end of the table, like he didn't want to sit directly next to either man, he needed space. It didn't look at all suspicious, but Eric knew he was being purposefully blocked in the corner. Charles didn't do anything by accident.

Charles did pretend to question Eric about the theft, but Eric could tell it was an act for Richards. Eric's answers were mostly grunted. His hands were shaking, so he squeezed them together in his lap, but couldn't stop his legs from bouncing under the table. It felt like the room was getting smaller, and Richards and Charles were taking up all the air. When the coffee grinder kicked on he jumped, knocked the bottom of the table and sent coffee splashing over the side of his cup. He tried to smile as Richards and Charles laughed about how he should probably lay off the coffee if it made him that jittery.

~~~~~

The doorbell tinkled as Kelly walked in, and as she rounded the corner, Mark waved. "Kelly! Glad you could join us! Look who we found. You know Eric, right?"

Eric was sitting at the table with Richards and Mark and looked...she couldn't even tell what was wrong with him. His pupils had constricted to tiny black dots in the center of his eyes, making the whites look too big. His smile was huge, exaggerated, extending all the way to his brow line. It looked like even his hair was smiling. But not in a friendly way. In a completely creepy, terrifying, Jack Nicholson in *The Shining* type of way.

She took an involuntary step backwards and bumped into another person. Hot coffee splashed all over her back.

"I'm so sorry," she said, turning, happy to have a reason not to be going to the table. Her hands were shaking as she grabbed napkins and tried to help mop up the mess. When she finally looked up, their eyes met. Ben smiled. She almost laughed. It was too ridiculous. "I'm so sorry."

"No worries. I've got another shirt in the car. It was in case I got dirty in the mine today, but...I guess I can use it now. Or I could keep the coffee stained shirt on until after. Either way, it's fine." He had taken his tie off, laid it on the counter and was gently mopping at the wet coffee on the end. "What are you doing here?"

Kelly looked at the table again, where all three men were watching her. Their eyes met, and she thought Eric was mouthing *"Leave!"* Mark was watching, the smile on his face fake and a little scary. She thought she saw him flexing his muscles under his shirt, as if he was trying to intimidate someone, but his eyes didn't meet hers.

"I had a quick meeting here, so I stayed at Mom and Dad's."

Ben nodded. "Actually, I'm glad I ran into you. Have you seen Joel's email?"

Kelly shook her head and tried to pull it up on her phone, but the screen froze trying to connect to the coffee shop's wireless connection.

Ben waved the hand holding the napkins. "It's okay, you don't have to read it now, all it says is that he didn't get anywhere with Burdock. The guy wouldn't even talk to him."

Kelly shook her head. "Dammit. That's not good."

Ben shook his head. "No, it really isn't. I'm afraid this is going to be even worse than we feared." He dropped the napkins in the garbage and looked around. "Where's Jordana?"

"Staying with my parents for the week."

"Listen, I've got to head out, I've got a meeting in Coleraine. Are you going to the office soon?"

"I was planning to stop at Grace first, but, yeah, I'll be there in a few hours."

"Okay. I'm stopping at Grace too, if we don't connect there, let's touch base this afternoon."

She looked at Eric again. Now he was mouthing *"Get out of here."*

She nodded slightly, not sure if Eric even noticed, then said goodbye to Ben and watched him leave before walking to the table.

"Hey, guys. I'm really sorry, but something came up. I've got to head to work. That was actually my boss."

"This will only take a minute. I've got just a few questions," Mark said.

Eric was subtly shaking his head and Kelly tried to avoid looking at him while she replied to Mark. "I'm really sorry. You've got my number. Give me a call later." She turned to Richards. "And, of course, you know how to get a hold of me." She looked at Eric over the top of Mark's head and tried to keep her face completely blank. "Eric. Good to see you again."

~~~~~

Eric exhaled a bit when she walked out, then fully when her car drove away. At least she was safe.

Richards stood. "I've got to head to the office." He reached across the table and shook Eric's hand. "It was good to see you again."

Eric stood. "I've got to take off too."

Charles didn't move. His face had the same maniacal smile that haunted Eric's nightmares. "Really good talking to you," he said. "I'm sure our paths will cross again soon."

~~~~~

From the coffee shop, Eric went to the office. He kept one eye on his rearview mirror the whole time, but following wasn't Charles's style. Charles liked surprise. The look in his eyes at the coffee shop was exactly the same pleasure he'd had when Eric walked in on him at the table at his grandparents' house.

He wished he had his pills with him, but they were still in the drawer at home. And the bag was almost empty. It was supposed to be his last one. He was getting clean. For Matt. And Kelly. But now, all he could think of was getting calm. He needed cash.

The receptionist wasn't at the office yet, and the few people who were at their desks were busy. No one looked up or noticed when he opened the locked drawer and shoved the money inside a zippered, blue, bank bag. The petty cash fund wasn't much, but it was enough. He took it all, relocked the safe and closed the drawer.

Nothing caught his eye as he drove around his apartment complex three times, but he didn't know what kind of vehicle he was looking for. When he finally parked, he ran from the car with the bank bag under his arm, got in as fast as he could, and flipped all the locks behind him. He even used the chain, which had never been put on the door and didn't easily slip into its slot. There was a hunting rifle on the living room wall and shells in the kitchen drawer. He took the gun down, loaded it, chambered a round, and went from room to room turning on lights and checking closets. He left every door open until he was satisfied there was no place for anyone to be hiding.

In the bedroom, he got the last two pills, took them to the kitchen where he mixed a Jack and Coke, and downed it all in one swig. He made a call and agreed to pay extra for home delivery. When the knock came, he had the exact amount of money in one hand and his rifle in the other.

The fisheye image seemed to swim at him through the peep hole. It wasn't Charles, so Eric flipped the deadbolt and latch lock. He left the chain on, handed the cash and accepted the zippered bag of pills in one movement through the slot.

"Eric, what's up?"

He didn't answer, just slammed the door and slid the locks back into place.

"What the fuck, man! You almost took my fingers off!"

Eric held the bag up and looked at its contents. The pills were mostly white, but there were a few small blue ones. Normally he would have asked what he got. Normally he would have placed a real order and demanded certain items. But this time wasn't normal. He didn't care.

~~~~~

Through her cell phone, Eric was screaming in Kelly's ear. She winced. She'd already tried to calm him down, to get him to speak in full sentences instead of expletives. But he wouldn't stop yelling. In her mind, she was picturing him jumping up and down like Jordana had done as a toddler, before she knew enough words to say what she meant. Frustrated, upset, and completely unreasonable. She told him to call her when he calmed down. He kept yelling. Finally, she had to hang up.

It was early afternoon before she made it to the office. She'd waited for Ben in Chisholm until he texted to tell her he was stuck in Coleraine. She wondered what he was working on there, or who he was meeting with, but didn't ask. If it affected her, he would share. Otherwise, it really wasn't any of her business.

The time in Chisholm wouldn't have been so bad if she could have spent some of it down in the Grace mine. She'd hoped to sneak in, but with the permits still in limbo, she was locked out. As were all the workers and essentially the whole project.

She'd just sat down at her desk when her cell rang again. "God dammit! Stop calling!" Even though she'd hissed the words through her teeth, it was a lot louder than she intended. She looked up, hoping no one had heard, but Mira was already coming into the office and closing the door.

"Can I talk to you?"

Kelly took a deep breath. "Of course. Sorry if you heard that."

"Are you okay?" Mira stood in front of Kelly's desk. She wasn't usually timid, but her voice was barely above a whisper, and, while she was meeting Kelly's eyes, the contact was uncomfortable.

"Yes. Sorry, I just—"

"No, it's not even what I just heard. I mean, that's part of it, but, honestly…" Mira took a deep breath. "You've been… I don't want you to think I'm judging you or anything. But you've been going back to Grand Rapids every weekend. Leaving work early, coming in late. There have been a lot of meetings…Is there something going on with Jordana's dad?"

Kelly sighed. "I'm okay. Jordana's father…he's…." She stopped herself from going into her rehearsed excuses and really looked at Mira. She'd been the first person Kelly hired at ReEarth, and she was the one who led the community interest meetings when they opened Grace. For that alone Kelly would forever be grateful to her. She was able to calm the irrational, screaming citizens, present the facts in an accessible, understandable manner, and even made herself available for follow-up questions. Her sweet mothering attitude was what had gotten the public support for that project in the first place. If Kelly had done those meetings herself…

Besides all that, she was an incredible scientist—able to both think up completely out-of-the-box hypotheses and also willing to change them when the evidence didn't line up.

She wasn't one of those people who pried into others' lives. She kept her head down and got her work done. But she was the one all the interns talked to about their college problems. She was also the one who ordered cakes and got cards signed every time someone got married or had a baby.

No one at ReEarth except Frank even knew Jordana's father was dead. It would be nice to have someone to talk to. Mira would understand.

"He's actually—"

There was a light knock on the door, and Ben's head poked through. "Sorry I missed you in Chisholm. You didn't wait too long, did you?"

Kelly shook her head.

"Yeah, there's really not much going on there. It's really frustrating. Anyway, are we still on for four o'clock?"

"Yes. But I don't have a lot done yet."

"That's okay. I'd like to see where we're at."

"Of course," Kelly said.

Ben nodded and pulled the door shut again.

The moment to confide was gone. "I'm sorry," Kelly said to Mira. "It's just some personal stuff. Jordana's dad is completely out of the picture; it's not that. I'm sorry it's been affecting my work."

"Oh, no," Mira held up her hands. "I don't think it's affecting your work at all. That's not what I was saying. I just...I could tell something's not right. I hope you don't mind that I asked. I thought...we've worked together so long...if you need a friend..." she looked at the floor, then at the door. "*I'm* sorry. It's none of my business."

Kelly smiled. "It's really okay. Thanks for asking."

Mira turned, and Kelly thought she was going to leave, but instead opened both doors, sat down and held up the tablet she'd had under her arm. "Are you ready to review the week?"

Kelly nodded. "Absolutely. Let's go."

Somehow, days went by. Eric didn't remember what he did during them, only the feeling of eyes on every inch of his skin. He was turning around at every sound. Whenever someone entered or exited the building he held the gun in his hands until he was sure the steps weren't coming toward his door. He left all the lights on and still felt the dark closing in.

He tried to call Kelly a few times, but something kept her from understanding. Damn cell phone reception. He asked her to drive back to Rapids and meet him, but she made up an excuse about work and said she would need to call back. He'd thought she'd figured it out at the coffee shop, but if she did, there was no sign of it now. He considered calling Richards, confessing everything just so he could tell him who McDonald really was. Even strung out, though, he knew it would never work.

~~~~~

Kelly wondered if she should call Sherrie, or even Eric's parents. Something was very, very wrong, and she didn't know what to do. But they were already there, already dealing with him, and she didn't want to seem like she was sticking her nose where it didn't belong. She had her own stuff to deal with.

Mark was calling her. A lot. It wasn't all about the shoes, and she didn't entirely mind. He seemed kind. Earnest. Really hell-bent on getting the shoes back, but because he wanted justice for the people of Grand Rapids—and, as he said, *"Wizard of Oz fans everywhere!"*

In all of Eric's incoherent ramblings the one thing she did understand was that he didn't want her talking to Mark at all. Even though it was probably jealousy, she'd trusted him for a long time, she couldn't completely discount him now. Those warnings were the one thing she kept coming back to, every time she started trying to plan a way for Mark to find the shoes.

~~~~~

Eric had been pacing around his apartment for hours taking deep breaths and practicing what he would say when she answered the phone. He needed to make her understand this time.

"You have to move," he said, cutting her off in the middle of *Hello.* "Now. Get the fuck out of Duluth."

"What? Why? Where should I go? You want me to come back to Grand Rapids?"

He could hear the sarcasm in her voice and shook his head. "No!" She wasn't getting it.

"Please calm down."

Shit. Now she was mad. "Sorry." He took another deep breath, then tried again. "You're not safe. You have to get out of here."

"What are you talking about?"

"He wants the shoes." Eric said the words slowly, deliberately, making sure she could understand exactly what he was saying.

"Who?"

"And his name isn't Mark. Remember when Jared got beat up? Said it was an ATV accident?"

"He told me it was a fight. But yeah, I heard later he was saying ATV. What's that have to do—"

"Charles beat him up." He was talking too fast now, his voice matching the pace of his steps. But the words, like his feet, wouldn't stop. "The guy that shot me and Brad. Charles. Mark is Charles."

"Eric, calm down. The guy that shot you, it was all connected to that meth ring. You were knocked out. You hallucinated. Those guys admitted to being in the mine."

He shook his head. Why didn't anyone ever believe him about the drug guys? They'd never even been charged with the crime, yet the whole town seemed to accept they'd done it, and whatever punishment they received was enough to prove their guilt. "They didn't admit to shooting anyone."

"They didn't have to. The plea bargain—"

"Fuck the plea!" His voice was rising, he was about to lose it. "I know what happened. I was there. I saw him shoot Brad. I was there!"

He stopped himself and took a breath. It was his last chance to save her. "You have to take your child and get out of there. Move somewhere. Change your name. Start over."

"I'm sorry, I've got to go."

"Kelly! Kelly!" He slammed the phone down and grabbed a pill out of his bag. The Jack Daniels was gone, as was his beer. And nearly everything else consumable in the apartment. The gun, still loaded, stood in the corner by the door.

Charles hadn't been by. He hadn't called. Eric had even been watching the parking lot. Nothing suspicious had happened.

He wished it was all a dream. Or one long drug-induced hallucination. But it was completely real. Charles had tried to kill him once. He wouldn't miss the second time. But Kelly...even if he couldn't save himself, he needed to save her.

He would figure out a way to make her understand.

He laid the gun on the coffee table and stretched out on the couch. He had to get some sleep, clear his mind enough to think.

Somehow, she had to believe him.

~~~~~~

He wasn't stable. She shouldn't have answered the phone—she had enough to deal with without this. There had been something very wrong with him ever since he was shot, and she wanted to be a friend, but this was going beyond.

It was almost eight p.m. and she was still at work. When Jordana was gone, sometimes she found it easier to stay at the office than take the laptop home to an empty apartment. But the silence was suddenly heavy. She tried to shake off what he'd said, but she couldn't rationalize it away. He'd never said she was in danger before.

The lake spread out below her window like a puddle of spilled blue paint in the twilight. There was no peace in it, either. The darkness, the way the lights shimmered off the surface but never seemed to be absorbed...it was how her life was starting to feel.

Eric couldn't call her since his cell was dead, so he tried knocking quietly. When there was no answer, he banged.

He was midway through another round of knocking when a little girl in wrinkled blue pajamas opened the door, rubbing her eyes. "Hey, you must be Jordana."

She nodded.

"Can you go wake your mom up?"

She nodded again and let go of the door. It slowly closed while Eric watched her walk down the hall.

~~~~~

Kelly heard the pounding as part of her dream, but didn't wake up. She'd been up late, listening to all of the adventures Jordana had while with her grandparents: four-wheeling in the woods, a trip to Itasca State Park to climb the old fire tower, and not one, but two trips to the movie theater.

"Mom? There's a guy at the door. He said he needs to talk to you."

Kelly jerked up in bed, everything Eric had said about Mark/Charles coming back to her like a slap to the face. What if he was right? She looked at the clock. It was ten to seven on Saturday morning. A time he could almost be certain she would be home, with her child.

"Stay in here," Kelly said.

"Who is it?"

"Lock the door."

There was another knock, and Kelly saw Jordana jump, her eyes growing bigger. Kelly tried her best to remain calm as she knelt down and smoothed hair away from Jordana's face. "I'm sorry. I didn't mean to scare you. Cartoons are on. Let me see who's at the door, then we'll get dressed and go get doughnuts, okay?"

TV in Mom's room was a rare treat and it worked. After the word "cartoons" Jordana had gotten the remote and jumped in bed, not caring what else was said.

Kelly grabbed a robe and wrapped herself in it, even though she was wearing a T-shirt and yoga pants. She wanted to remind Jordana to lock the door, but she didn't want to scare her again.

The knocking got louder and Kelly hissed "Stop it! I'm coming."

She heard another door open and Mrs. McAlester's voice, then Eric apologizing.

Kelly yanked the door open. "I'm sorry, Mrs. McAlester."

"No problem." The old woman smiled kindly. "I was already up. I have fresh banana bread here if you want some?"

Kelly smiled. "Thanks, but I promised Jordana we'd go get doughnuts later."

"I'll take a slice," Eric said.

Kelly watched him, incredulous, as he stood in Mrs. McAlester's doorway while she cut and wrapped half a loaf. Mrs. McAlester caught Kelly's eye while Eric was thanking her. Kelly couldn't read the look there, so she tried to ignore it and let Eric into the apartment far enough for the door to close behind him. "What do you want? Do you know what time it is? You scared the crap out of us." He was leaning against the doorjamb, his shirt and jeans wrinkled, like they'd been worn for a few days. There were bags under his eyes and the start of a beard. She was surprised to see all the white hairs coming from his chin.

"I had to make sure you were okay." He unwrapped the bread and broke a piece off, letting the crumbs fall to the floor.

She sighed and led him to the table. He wasn't exactly stumbling, but he didn't seem completely stable.

"Why wouldn't we be okay?"

"Charles. You have to believe me. He—"

She cut him off as she pulled a canister out of the cupboard. "I need coffee. And keep your voice down. Jordana is in my room watching TV."

Her nose was filled with conflicting smells. The brewing coffee, banana bread, and a little bit of last night's garlic still wafted through the air. Eric smelled mostly like cigarettes and sweat, but there was also a sweet, almost antiseptic, smell coming from him. She recognized it, but it took her a few minutes to place. Whisky. Jack Daniels.

His eyes were red, but not completely bloodshot. He didn't seem so much drunk as sleep deprived.

"You want some?"

He nodded and she saw his legs bouncing under the table.

She set two mugs of coffee on the table and sat down across from him.

He wrapped his hands around his drink, but didn't pick it up. Instead, he stared at the liquid and said, "I promise you. This guy is Charles. He's the guy that beat Jared up. He killed Jared and Brad, and he tried to kill me. I thought, because his truck stayed at Grandma and Grandpa's...I hoped...but, well, you know he didn't get lost in the mine, you've been in there. I don't know how he got out, or where he's been. But he's back." He exhaled and looked up.

"Has he tried to contact you again?" A small part of her was worried about the possibility that what Eric was saying really was true, but none of it added up. If this was the guy that had killed two—almost three—people for the shoes, where had he been all these years?

And how would he have gotten the cops to cooperate with him? Besides, she'd vetted his company. He was a legit investigator. And, while intimidating, he certainly didn't seem like a killer.

"He looks different now. More built. He was a skinny little thug before. Powerful, but not…I don't know…I can't describe it. But it's him. Same eyes. Same face. I've had nightmares about that face for—"

Kelly put her hand over his and he stopped talking. She wasn't mad anymore, she felt sorry for him. He needed a help she couldn't give. "Have you talked to Richards?"

He stared. "Of course not. What would I say? 'Hey, so I actually helped Jared hide the shoes after he stole them, and I knew where they were. But when I tried to get them, I found out my cousin had already been there and taken them, and then this guy tried to kill me.' You know what the first thing he would say is? 'Why didn't you tell us this before?' And then they would charge me with interfering with the investigation. Or they wouldn't believe me at all. Like you don't."

"It's not that I don't believe you." The words were out of Kelly's mouth before she considered whether or not lying was the best course of action. "I just…I don't understand why he would show up after all this time."

"It's because of the mines. He must think they're still there, I guess."

"But we've been in Grace for years now. We would have found them—"

"Then I can't tell you!"
Kelly flinched.

Eric lowered his voice. "I don't know where he's been. But I know you're not safe. Back then…the things he said about you…You've got to go somewhere."

"I feel safe here." But it wasn't entirely true. "How did you get my address, anyway?"

"I told your mom I wanted to send you an invitation to our company picnic."

"Well, that's a little creepy. You could have asked me."

Eric shrugged, not at all apologetic. "I was afraid you wouldn't give it to me."

"Mom? Can I come out?"

Eric and Kelly's heads swiveled to the bedroom door. Kelly didn't want to offend Eric, but she was worried about what he might say in front of the child. He answered for her though. "Yeah, it's fine. I'm an old friend of your mom and dad's."

Kelly glared at him.

"You knew my dad?" Jordana practically ran to the table.

Kelly was relieved when he seemed to read the look in her eyes.

"No, sorry. I haven't had enough coffee yet this morning. I meant I'm an old friend of your mom's."

Kelly stopped holding her breath.

"Why are you here so early? You woke us up."

Eric shrugged. "I get up really early. Sometimes I forget other people don't."

Jordana turned to Kelly. "I'm hungry."

"Get yourself some cereal and take it back in my room, okay? I need to talk to Eric for a few more minutes."

Jordana nodded. While she got her cereal, Kelly silently prayed Eric wouldn't speak and was again surprised when he seemed to understand.

"Joey knew about Charles," Eric said, as soon as the bedroom door closed behind Jordana.

"Who?"

"Joey. Ostberg. Remember? His parents lived a few miles from Grandma and Grandpa's."

"Yeah, I remember. What's he have to do with anything?"

"You don't know?" Eric cocked his head and looked sideways at Kelly.

"Know what?"

She looked at the bedroom door again, hoping Jordana wasn't listening, debating whether to kick Eric out. She was sick of the back and forth, but hearing him out seemed like it might be the only way to get him to stop stalking her.

"Holy shit. You don't know." He lowered his voice and looked at the bedroom door. "Didn't Jared tell you anything?"

"What did he tell you?" Kelly was measuring her answers as she'd always done when asked about Jared. It had become an unconscious habit, never sharing more information than the other party had or could easily find out on their own. It seemed like a good policy, it had kept her out of jail, and real, legal suspicion this long.

"Nothing. Well, not much. I figured most of it out myself. But Joey confirmed it."

"What does Joey have to do with anything?"

Eric leaned close. "He hired Jared."

Kelly almost spit out her coffee. "What?" She'd known Joey since the first time she'd gone to Eric's grandparents' house. They'd played together as kids and ended up at a lot of the same parties in middle and high school.

Eric nodded. "I figured Joey'd introduced you guys."

"No. How did you know?"

"I heard them fighting one night. I was at Jared's, he was on the phone, freaking out about Hurricane Katrina." He watched her while he sipped his coffee.

She wanted to look away, to break eye contact, but couldn't.

"You really didn't know about this?"

She shook her head.

"Did Joey know about Jordana?"

"I don't know. I haven't talked to him."

"When was the last time?"

"I talked to him?" The swirling tobacco stains on the corner of the ceiling, left from some previous tenant, seemed to be beckoning her. She could bum one from Eric. But when Jordana was in kindergarten they'd taught her cigarettes were a drug that caused cancer and people died from cancer. All true, but not something a teacher should tell a five-year-old whose mom is a smoker. Jordana had cried nearly every day until Kelly quit. "I don't remember," she finally said.

"Did he know you had Jared's kid?"

"Shut up," she hissed.

"She is, right?" Eric whispered.

Kelly nodded. "I still don't understand though. Joey hired…"

"Jared. To steal—"

Kelly cut him off with her eyes and gestured toward the door. They could hear the TV, but they both knew that didn't mean Jordana wasn't trying to eavesdrop.

"Listen. You and I need to talk. Privately."

"She's going to a friend's house at noon."

He stood and downed the last of his coffee. "Great. I'll be back then."

He walked out with more confidence and composure than he'd arrived with. There was something convincing about the change in his attitude. Kelly was starting to believe him.

~~~~~

In the car on the way back from dropping Jordana off, Kelly called Sherrie. It took a lot of small talk—about the kids, their jobs, being single mothers—before Kelly felt like she could say why she'd called. "I'm worried about Eric."

"Really?" Sherrie was washing dishes, Kelly could hear them clinking in the background. "Why?"

"He's just..." she tried to remember what Sherrie already knew. "Have you heard a private investigator is working on finding the Ruby Slippers?"

"Yeah, it was all over the news here for weeks."

"Mmhmm. I've been questioned again—"

"That's ridiculous! Just because you dated the guy doesn't mean you had anything to do with it!"

Kelly made a noise to indicate she appreciated Sherrie's support. "Eric's been kind of freaking out about it," she said. "He says he's worried about me, my safety..."

Sherrie sighed. "Just a minute." She must have put her hand over the receiver, because the next thing Kelly heard was a muffled "Matt, go outside and play now. You've watched enough TV." There was some complaining, a short negotiation, and Kelly heard a door creak and close.

"Okay," Sherrie said into the phone. "Sorry about that. I don't like him to hear me talking about Eric."

Kelly was about to say she understood, but Sherrie continued.

"Eric's not well. He's been a bit...I don't want to say paranoid, but I can't think of another word for it... since he was shot. He still thinks they're out to get him."

Kelly decided to play dumb. "Even with all the stuff about the meth dealers? Does he think they're coming after him when they get out of jail?"

"No, he never believed they did it. He told the cops too, that's why there weren't formal charges filed. The guys were already going to jail, it was easy to pin on them. Eric says he knows who did it, but if he ever told, the guy would come back to finish the job."

Kelly nodded and tried to figure out what else to say.

"He doesn't get overnights with Matt anymore. He's not even supposed to be alone with him, but I let them go fishing sometimes. It's just...I don't want Matt to know there is anything wrong with his dad, but I'm afraid that one day Eric's going to go off the deep end. Plus, the drinking is always worse at night. I made up some excuse a long time ago and Eric's never questioned it."

"I'm sorry," Kelly said.

"Me too. I will say this, though: he pays his child support. Which is more than a lot of single mothers have. So I'm thankful for that. Hang on."

Kelly heard the door creak again and a muffled conversation. "I've got to go. But let me know next time you're in Rapids. We can let our parents watch the kids and go get a glass of wine."

"I'd like that," Kelly said.

~~~~~

"Hi, sweetie. Are you okay?"

Kelly spun around and tried to not look alarmed. Mrs. McAlester must have been watching through her peephole, because Kelly'd barely had time to reach into her purse for her apartment keys. "Yeah, why?"

"Well, that boy this morning…was he bothering you? He seemed nice enough, and I don't want to put my nose where it doesn't belong, but I wanted to check."

Kelly tried to smile. "Thank you. He's an old friend, going through a hard time. We're okay, though."

"Is he…" she let her voice drift off and seemed to be trying to look through Kelly's closed door. "Jordana's father?" She barely spoke the words audibly but over-exaggerated her facial movements so Kelly could read her lips.

Kelly shook her head. "He's dead." Since almost telling Mira, she'd decided there was no reason to keep trying to hide it; it didn't make her or Jordana's life any easier for people to think there was a deadbeat dad somewhere out there.

Mrs. McAlester put a hand over her heart. "I'm so sorry."

"It's okay. He died right after I found out I was pregnant."

"That's terrible. Does Jordana know?"

Kelly nodded. "She doesn't know who he was, but I told her last year that he was dead. She's old enough for that much information. I know soon she's going to want details—" Kelly saw Eric approaching out of the corner of her eye and pulled her keys out. "I've got to get going."

"Oh, of course. But, Kelly? I want you to know… You're raising an amazing girl there, and working so hard. And I am happy to help you any way I can." She stepped forward and put a hand on Kelly's shoulder, and Kelly allowed herself to be pulled into a hug. It was warm and comfortable and Kelly wished she could stay there where the worst thing in her life was that Jordana didn't have a father.

But then Eric was beside her, looking impatient. She pulled away. "Thank you."

~~~~~

Eric nodded at Mrs. McAlester, who wasn't even trying to hide the curiosity on her face, and followed Kelly into the apartment. As soon as the door closed behind him he said, "We're going to call Joey." He'd had time to take a quick nap in his car and formulate a plan. "I need to plug this in." He held up his cell phone and the charger.

"Hello, again," she said.

"Sorry. Hi."

"We're going to call Joey," he said again. It was a long shot—he was almost sure Joey was dead, but verifying would be its own kind of proof. And if Joey was alive, he could confirm everything for Kelly. "He can explain it all to you. And he'll tell you: Mark really is Charles."

She nodded and pointed at an outlet under the table.

Eric plugged his phone in and waited for the screen to light up, then hit a few buttons. "Give me your phone."

"Why?"

"This might die. Just give it to me."

She handed over her cell, he dialed the number and turned on the speaker.

It was answered the first ring. "Yeah."

Eric sank heavily into the chair. He hadn't truly considered what it would be like to hear Joey's voice. He clenched and unclenched his hands, trying to fight through relief and anger and suspicion to get to the words. Joey was still alive.

"Hello?" Joey said again.

Eric swallowed. "Joey. It's Eric. I'm at Kelly's. You're on speaker."

"Hey," she said. Her voice came out soft and meek, and when Eric looked at her she blushed and pretended to cough.

Had there been something between the two of them, too? Maybe she was the reason Joey'd stopped calling. Maybe she'd *told* him—

"Kelly?" Joey asked.

"Kelly Martin," Eric said.

"No shit! How are you?"

"I'm good." There was a little more strength in her voice.

"What have you been up to? You two together now? Where you living?" he paused for a second, but before they could answer, he continued. "Why are you calling me on speaker? Only my parents do this. What's up?"

"Joey." Eric was working hard to sort through all of the voices in his head, all of the things he wanted to say. "You need to tell Kelly about Jared."

Joey laughed, but Eric knew it was fake. "What are you talking about? Jared who?"

"Don't fuck with us." Eric fought the urge to pick the phone up and yell into it. "Charles is here. In town."

There was no response. Kelly started to reach for the phone, but Eric held up a finger for her to wait. Finally, Joey sighed. "Are you sure?"

"Yes. And I wouldn't be calling you, but I don't think Kelly's safe."

"What's going on?" Joey asked.

Eric filled him in. "He looks different, but, man, I know it's him."

"Let me look into it," Joey said. "I'll get back to you."

"Wait!" Eric grabbed the phone off the table. "You have to tell her. Tell Kelly you knew Jared."

Eric locked eyes with her and held the phone out. Joey sighed again. "Yeah. Yeah, I knew him. Met him down here."

"And you hired him," Eric prompted. He wasn't going to let there be any confusion.

"It wasn't like that," Joey said. "I—"

"I don't want to know any more," Kelly said. She hit the red circle to disconnect the call.

Eric stood and paced around until he was under control enough to speak without yelling at her. She shouldn't have hung up. There was more he'd wanted to say. "Do you believe me now?"

She didn't answer, just got up and began pacing herself. In the kitchen, she paused, holding the counter, not looking at him. Then, standing on her tiptoes, she reached into the cabinet above the refrigerator and pulled out a bottle of brandy, poured a little more than a shot each into two tumblers and set them on the table. "Yeah," she finally said, then tilted her head back and downed the liquor.

Eric looked at his glass. He could taste the sweet burn, but he kept his arms crossed. He needed to maintain this clarity as long as he could. Kelly used one finger to push it toward him; when he shook his head she picked it up and drank it.

"I knew he would come back for me. No one believed me. But I was right. He's here now," he said.

"But he made no attempt to contact you. He only came after me."

"He knew I was in love with you." It wasn't something he'd planned on saying, but he didn't mind when the words came out. She must have known.

"Eric. We can't—"

"Then. I was in love with you then." He took one of the empty tumblers to the sink, rinsed it and filled it with water that he drank in one gulp, and filled it again. "I know…" He went and stood at the window. "I don't know why he came to you instead of me. I don't know why he left you alone back then. I do know he's dangerous. We've got to figure something out."

She chewed on her nail. "I need to smoke," she said finally. "You coming?"

~~~~~

They stood at the corner of the building and smoked in silence, letting nicotine fill their blood streams. By the time they went back inside, Eric was sure Kelly not only understood what was really going on, but actually *believed* everything he'd been trying to say. The relief of it left him exhausted. He fell asleep on the couch while she was in the bathroom and she let him stay there until it was time to pick up Jordana.

"You going to be okay getting home?" She asked.

He rubbed his eyes and stretched like a child, then nodded.

"Lock the door behind you."

"Okay."

~~~~~

Eric couldn't drive all the way back to Grand Rapids, but he couldn't stay at Kelly's, not with Jordana. Besides the fact that she wouldn't let him, his hands had started shaking. He needed something.

There were no other cars when he pulled into the back of the mall parking lot, but he could see everyone who entered. The hunting rifle was lying across the back seat, unloaded, the bullets in the cup holder next to him. It wouldn't take long to load if he needed to.

Eventually a car idled slowly by, circled the lot a few times, and came back. Eric saw that it was high school kids, relaxed a little and threw a jacket over the gun.

"You buying?" the driver asked through the cracked window.

"What do you have?"

"Oxy."

Eric nodded and handed a twenty-dollar bill through the window. In return, a single pill was placed in his hand. "Come on, man."

The kid shrugged. "That's a pretty good deal, actually. I don't know you. I could have cut it in half."

Eric looked in his wallet. There wasn't enough to buy more and still get gas to make it home. He started the car, flipped the kids off, and peeled out of the lot, the pill already dissolving in his mouth. He held it there as long as he could stand before swallowing.

He didn't really have anywhere to go, so he drove down to the lake and parked where he could see the waves crashing against the rocky shore. The Oxy was enough to take the edge off, barely, and it made him itch for more. But at least the shaking had stopped.

~~~~~

Kelly's phone buzzed while she was driving, but she let it go. She'd made a promise to Jordana not to text and drive, and, while she definitely didn't have an unblemished record, she was making a conscious effort to cut back. And she already felt guilty for smoking.

If Mark was Charles, and he had killed Jared and Brad…her hand hovered over the phone as she thought about calling Detective Richards. But it wouldn't do any good. Mark or Charles or whatever his name was obviously had Richards in his pocket already.

The shoes were still in the trunk of her car. She needed to move them, but she didn't know where to put them. She'd confirmed that Eric and Mark were right about the statute of limitations, but there was no good way to clean her prints. It would be impossible to prove she'd just found them. She could still be charged with harboring stolen goods.

She pulled the car up in front of Sarah's house and checked her reflection in the mirror. There were bags under her eyes, even though she'd slept well. At least until Eric showed up. Her hair was greasy in the front, the result of running her hands through it so many times this morning. And she hadn't showered. She'd put on mascara, so at least her eyes looked open, but no other makeup. There was nothing to do about it now.

She left the phone in the cup holder, purposefully not checking the message in case it was Jordana asking for more time.

~~~~~

Sarah and Jordana had met in kindergarten, and this was the first year they didn't have class together. Jordana talked all the way home about Sarah's crush on the new boy, Jeremy, how cute he was…

Kelly let Jordana's chatter blend into background noise, like the music coming out of the radio. She did her best to be an attentive mother, but sometimes Jordana talked to hear her own voice. She'd done it ever since she first learned how to make sounds. She'd been the noisiest, happiest baby ever. Not much had changed as she'd grown. She was still rattling on as she bounced up the stairs and into their apartment. Without the key.

Dammit, Eric. If he was so worried about her safety, why didn't he lock the door?

Inside, Kelly tried to shake the uneasy feeling of someone lurking, watching her. The unlocked door was Eric's carelessness, nothing more. She pulled her phone out to text him and saw the message.

Is it this guy? There was a picture of someone who looked very similar to Mark from a number she didn't recognize.

Who is this? She typed back.

Joey. The reply was almost immediate.
Looks like him. But Mark is more built.

She waited for a response but didn't get one. She hoped it wasn't wishful thinking to take the silence as confirmation that Mark and Charles were not the same person.

~~~~~

That night, after Jordana was asleep, Kelly drank most of a bottle of wine while watching TV and had an epiphany. What if Mark and Charles *weren't* the same person? What if they were *brothers?*

The revenge angle was more intriguing and believable, but also much more frightening. If Charles really had died somewhere in that mine…

But he couldn't have. They would have found his body by now. Those tunnels, they had all been expanded and reinforced. If there was a body down there, even if it'd been somehow buried, they'd smell it. But what if he hadn't died *in* the mine. What if he'd gotten out, and something had happened to him in the woods? They weren't commonly sighted, but the black bears and moose living there weren't friendly. Plus, there were timberwolves. And cougars. If he'd gotten out of the mine, but been hurt…his body could have easily been devoured.

She shivered and pulled her blanket tighter. It was the wine and the movie. She needed to go to bed. With the TV off and the apartment silent, she could hear her upstairs neighbors walking around, and rather than be annoyed by their late night movements, tonight she took comfort in knowing they were there. She made sure the door was locked and thought about her footfalls registering to the people below her. She was safe. Jordana was safe. But she had to get rid of the shoes. Tomorrow. If she didn't have them anymore, there would be no reason for anyone to come after her.

Mrs. McAlester had snuck into the apartment at quarter to six, given Kelly a hot blueberry muffin and hug and sat down at the table with her paper.

It was time to take care of the shoes. Kelly pulled into a spot at the back of the ReEarth parking lot and made sure there was no one else around before getting out of her car and going to the trunk. From where she was standing she could see if anyone entered the lot, but there wasn't much risk. Even the earliest people didn't show up before seven.

The click of the rubber box's lid opening echoed in the empty morning air. The breeze coming off the lake gave her goose bumps. She tried not to shiver as she reached in with two gloved hands and lifted the backpack onto the tarp covering the inside of her trunk.

"Hi, there." The familiar voice behind her made her jump. She tried to take a deep breath and remain calm as she looked up and over the car, desperately wishing to see someone else coming in way too early on a Monday morning.

But there wasn't another vehicle in sight.

She slowly turned, trying to keep her body in front of the backpack she'd been about to carry into the office. She was going to find a box, seal it up, and address it to the Grand Rapids Police Department. Then she was going to put stamps—regular old postage stamps, enough to cover the shipping costs—on the box and leave it at a Post Office somewhere on the Iron Range. She hadn't decided which yet; she was still trying to figure out where it would be least likely anyone would come up with any connection to her. She'd arranged to collect soil samples from as many old mine sites along the Range as she could hit in a day, putting her in the vicinity of at least a dozen post offices, plus all the businesses that would accept outgoing packages. She hadn't decided what to do about possible fingerprints yet, other than pray there weren't any on the shoes. Prints on the backpack would be easy to explain, she had dated Jared, after all.

"Beautiful morning, isn't it?" Mark was leaning against the brick building across the alley from ReEarth's parking lot. He wasn't there when she pulled in. He couldn't have been. She would have seen him.

"Hi." She reached up with one hand to shut the trunk, but it caught on the rubber box.

A water bottle was attached to his palm with an elastic strap, he lifted it to his lips and took a long drink. Sweat was dripping off his forehead and he pulled the hem of his tank top up to wipe it away.

She couldn't not look at his well-defined stomach muscles, or the way his mesh shorts clung precariously to his hip bones. Part of her wanted to reach out and touch him. The other part wanted to turn and run.

He smiled. "I didn't mean to scare you. I was out for my morning run and saw your car pull in."

She cocked her head, but he answered her question before she asked it.

"Yeah. I run from the harbor to Central High… or what used to be Central High…twice a week." He smiled and wiped away the sweat from his forehead again. "It sucks."

She looked up the hill to the old school building and almost forgot that she was trying to hide the backpack behind her.

"I can't stay long. But I do still have questions. It's been a while… everything okay with work? I know you guys have been having some problems…"

She shook her head and shifted her weight to the other foot. "It's fine."

He nodded and took another drink of water, then fiddled with the bottle's strap. "Can we set up a meeting—"

The bottle suddenly dropped and rolled to Kelly's feet. She bent to pick it up, realizing her mistake a moment too late.

"What do you have in there?" he asked.

She leaned against the car as nonchalantly as possible and held out the bottle. "Just work stuff."

He nodded and crossed his arms, suddenly very intimidating. She forgot completely about his abs as the muscle in his jaw worked. "It's the same kind of backpack they say Jared had. And it's old. Why do you have such an old bag?"

Kelly shrugged. "I don't know. I just—"

"His was never found. Everyone we talked to confirmed it was with him all the time. To have it be gone when his apartment was searched...there is a strong chance the Ruby Slippers were hidden in it."

Kelly stepped back, but ended up sitting awkwardly on the lip of the trunk. She tried to sound thoughtful. "I think I remember it."

"You do. I have confidence in you."

Kelly heard the sound of a diesel engine gearing down on the road past the office, and followed Mark's eyes over her shoulder. Ben. Thank God.

Mark looked at his watch, feigned surprise, and said, "I've got to get going if I'm going to make it to the school and back to my car. We'll talk soon." His eyes locked onto hers for a moment as he reached out and squeezed her shoulder, just hard enough to hurt. "Very soon."

Ben parked his truck next to Kelly's car and was hopping out as she slammed the trunk.

"Who was that?"

"Old friend."

"What the hell is he doing?"

"He runs from the harbor to the school twice a week, I guess."

Ben shook his head. "That's crazy."

Kelly faked a smile. "Yeah. Nuts."

"You going in?"

Kelly nodded and followed him, even though she was going to need to go back and get the shoes soon—before Mark had time to come back.

*M*ark McDonald is Charles.

The four word text from Joey came right at the end of a staff meeting and made Kelly sink into the chair across from her desk. She stared at the words, waiting for a follow-up *not* that never came. *Mark McDonald is Charles* stayed on the screen, screaming at her.

It had been nearly a month with no word from Joey. Eric had told her to wait, but even he seemed to be backing off a little. Mark had left a few messages asking to meet again, but she had used the craziness at ReEarth as an excuse. He'd been so polite—he hadn't come back and tried to break into her car or even asked her any more about the backpack—and the radio silence from Joey had started to make her feel safe. Not safe enough to move the shoes, but….

She walked to the lab where Mira and Joel were working. "Jordana's sick. I've got to go get her."

"I'm sorry," Joel said.

"I'll get her settled at home and should be back online within an hour."

They nodded.

She packed up her computer, stopped by Ben's office on her way to the door and told him the same lie.

The heat in her car was sweltering, but she didn't dare roll the windows down. The doors were locked. "I need help," she said as soon as Joey answered the phone.

She told him about finding the shoes, how she wanted to give them back, and about Mark seeing the backpack in her car the morning she'd tried to mail them.

"Does Eric know?"

"No."

"And what were you going to do?"

She told him her plan to mail them.

"It's never going to work."

"Well, I'm sorry. Not all of us are professional criminals."

The line was silent.

"I'm sorry. I'm stressed." *And hot. And people are going to start to wonder why I'm still sitting in the parking lot while my sick daughter wastes away at school.* She started the car and pulled out, driving with her left hand so she could use her right to hold the phone.

Joey laughed. "I'm glad you've gotten a little of your sass back. I've missed that. But let's be clear. Neither am I."

"Sass? Are you my grandmother?"

"Just trying to talk proper, since you're a mother now."

"Properly."

"Whatever. I meant that I'm trying not to cuss your ear off."

"You can swear as much as you want as long as you can help me."

"Sit tight. I'll see what I can do."

"Am I safe?" She didn't know how Joey could guarantee his answer, but she wanted to hear it anyway.

"You will be. I've got to make some calls. Until you hear from me don't talk to Charles."

"You mean Mark?"

"Him, either."

~~~~~

Eric called Kelly. "I'll be at your place at six. We're picking Joey up at the airport at six-thirty. Find some place for Jordana to spend the night."

~~~~~

Kelly was on the couch. Her computer, on the coffee table in front of her, kept beeping to let her know she had new messages. Mira was sending her new information from Minnesotans for Minerals, and Ben was IMing her.

She held her head in her hands, trying to figure out how it had gotten this bad. Was she really trying to hide her daughter?

She straightened up, scrolled through numbers on the phone, and found Elizabeth, Sarah's mom. *I've got a work issue. Could Jordana spend the night at your place tonight? I'll take the kids one day this weekend so you and Evan can have a date.*

Another email popped up. Kelly read the preview quickly and yanked the computer into her lap. She clicked the attachment, and barely noticed the reply from Elizabeth on her phone. *Yes.*

Minnesotans for Minerals were calling for *prosecution*. Criminal charges, to be brought against "individuals, including but not limited to, Benjamin Ward, Kelly Martin, Frank Gustofsen, and Daniel Kaur." The words "willful destruction of natural resources" and "toxic contamination" jumped out at her.

The phone rang. "Ben."

"Are you okay?"

"This is bull," she said.

"I know. I'm not panicking. I wanted to make sure you weren't."

"I'm not."

"Good. What have you got?"

"We've got the data, and everything's been redone. We're fine. I just...I have to figure out how to prove ours is real and theirs isn't."

"Okay. Well, no pressure, but..."

"Yeah. I know. I'm going as fast as I can."

"How's Jordana?"

"What?"

"Jordana. Is she feeling any better?"

Kelly closed her eyes. She'd almost forgotten the lie she'd told about why she was home. "Yeah. She's doing a little better."

"Good. Let me know if you need anything."

"Okay."

She spent the afternoon on the phone and the computer, half her attention focused on reading and interpreting data, the other half directing Mira and Joel and discussing PR moves with Nicole. It was almost three before she remembered to call the school. First, she had to tell the office secretary Jordana was going home with a friend, then she had to tell Jordana's teacher, and, finally, Jordana had to be pulled out of her reading group so Kelly could tell her. Jordana was thrilled, but everyone else was obviously annoyed by the last minute arrangements. Kelly understood why parents gave kids cell phones. Calling Jordana directly would have been so much easier.

She changed quickly out of her work clothes into jeans and a t-shirt, and took a shot of brandy as Eric knocked on the door.

~~~~~

The drive to the airport was almost silent. They pulled up to the curb where Joey was waiting, popped the trunk, and waited while he climbed into the car.

"Nice gun you got back there," Joey said.

Eric nodded.

"Why do you have a gun?" Kelly asked.

Eric shrugged. "Ducks."

Joey said, "I'm starving. Let's go to the mall."

"Why the mall?" Eric asked.

"Food court."

Kelly laughed and turned in her seat to look at Joey. "Are you sixteen?"

"We're less likely to be noticed there than if we go to a restaurant." His eyes were deadly serious.

Kelly turned back around and stared out the windshield. This wasn't going to be a fun reunion.

~~~~~

"I want the museum to get them back," Kelly said.

Eric took a big bite of his burger.

Joey nodded. "That's fine. But we've got to be smart about it." He was eating french fries and a gyro, the sandwich's white sauce dripped down the side of his hand.

"Do you promise?" Kelly hated how powerless she felt. Eric wouldn't look at her, staring instead at his food like he hadn't eaten in days. "And what about Mark? Charles. Whatever his name is. What's he going to do?"

"I've got him," Joey said. "You've got two options. One, we could dump the shoes somewhere they'd be easily found. It would have to be in Grand Rapids, so there would be no question about what they are or what should be done with them."

Kelly nodded. So far, she was with him.

"Or, two, you can give them to me. Let me take care of everything."

Kelly shook her head. "I can't. I need to—"

Joey held up his hand. "I figured you'd say that. Here's what's going to happen, then. Eric's going to drive me back to Rapids tonight."

Eric looked up when Joey said his name, but didn't say anything.

"You need to meet us over there tomorrow," Joey continued. "In the park by the Mississippi. The one by the library? Across from Blandin?"

"Why?" Kelly asked.

"It's a good place for the drop. We can watch to see who finds them and make sure they're turned in."

Kelly thought about it for a minute. She was going to have to miss work again. But she couldn't think of any better plan. And, this way, she was getting rid of the shoes. Finally.

"Unless, of course, you want to give them to me," Joey offered again.

Kelly faked a smile and tried not to wonder why he was pushing so hard to get the shoes. "No, thanks."

He nodded and finished the last of his sandwich. "Let's get going," he said to Eric. "Kelly's got some packing to do."

~~~~~

Eric spent most of the drive to Grand Rapids trying to figure out why Kelly had told Joey she had the shoes and not him. Why didn't she trust him, even after all he'd done for her? There was no reason. He was pissed.

On the north side of the city Joey asked about Eric's stash. He admitted it was almost depleted, and Joey directed him to pull into an abandoned parking lot. "They still sell here?"

"Yeah, but I'm out of money," Eric said.

"No problem." Joey punched Eric in the shoulder. "I got you."

Within five minutes another car pulled up. Joey got out and went to the other vehicle. Eric couldn't see who it was, but Joey seemed to know them. He shook hands first, then leaned down and rested his elbows on the passenger door. Eric could hear talking and laughing but wasn't really listening to what they were saying. He half-heartedly scanned the road, watching for cop cars.

Not that there was much chance of getting caught. If the cops cared, they'd stake someone out here. They didn't.

When he got back in the car, Joey was smiling. He waved the baggie of white, blue, yellow and pink candy-like pills at Eric. "You have anything to drink?"

Eric shook his head.

"Shit, man. Seriously? Alright. Let's hit the liquor store too."

By the time they got back to Eric's apartment he was sweating and shaking, but it wasn't withdrawal. It was like he could feel Charles's presence, even though there was no sign of him anywhere. He circled the parking lot twice, ignoring Joey's growing annoyance. At the door, he had to concentrate to get the key into the lock and turn it.

"What the fuck, man?" Joey followed him in. "No one ever taught you to shut lights off? Or close doors?"

Eric shrugged and threw his keys on the counter. The apartment was exactly as it had been for the last several weeks. He'd never thought about what it might look like to another person. He'd left the gun in the trunk and wanted to go back to get it, but there was something about having a loaded gun in his apartment with Joey that seemed worse than being unarmed.

Joey dropped his duffle bag on the floor and laid the candy bag on the counter.

"What happened to you?" Eric asked.

Joey avoided Eric's eyes while he fished out two blue capsules. "What do you mean?"

Eric accepted one of the pills, but held it in his hand. "You stopped calling. I thought you…I mean… Charles…" Eric couldn't get the words out.

Joey shrugged. "I thought it was over." He freed the liquor from its brown sleeve, poured drinks, handed one to Eric, and raised his glass. "To the fucking Ruby Slippers."

It wasn't enough. Eric wanted more: to know where the hell Joey'd been all this time; why he'd dropped off the face of the planet; what exactly he was planning to do with the shoes. Even just an assurance he was going to keep Kelly safe. But Eric knew he wasn't going to get any of those things, and pressing could be dangerous, so he put the pill under his tongue and washed it down with the shot.

While Joey was in the bathroom, Eric pulled a few more tablets out of the bag, wrapped them in a paper towel, and shoved them in his pocket. He was sitting in front of the TV when Joey came out. "So what's the real plan?"

Joey shook his head. "The less you know, the better."

Eric wanted to argue, but his head was too light to form full thoughts. And his body had melted into the couch. He closed his eyes, just for a second.

~~~~

"I'll get them to you." Joey's muffled voice blended in and out of an infomercial about face creams.

Eric fought to open his eyes and the silence stretched long enough he thought he'd been dreaming. But then Joey said, "I have no idea. I didn't ask for details," and Eric realized he was on the phone.

Eric shifted a little, his body was still heavy, but the fog in his brain cleared slightly.

"No, I don't know if she's seen them...What difference does it make? If she doesn't have them, you're no worse off than you are now...Let's not forget, I already—No. No. I'm sorry...Yes...We'll be in touch."

The bedroom door creaked open and Eric leaned back and closed his eyes.

"Wake up," Joey shoved Eric's shoulder much harder than necessary. "I want to sleep, and I'm not doing it in your dirty ass sheets. Get some clean ones."

Eric pretended to have a hard time waking up, and faked looking around in confusion, but the way he stumbled on the way to the bedroom was completely real. There was a set of flannel sheets in the closet and a sleeping bag, he threw them on the bed and took his pillow and comforter before going back out to the couch.

He drifted in and out of sleep, waiting until he was sure Joey was out, then got up and dialed Kelly's number.

"He's not going to give them back," Eric hissed when she answered. His voice was too high, too fast, even to his own ears. He didn't sound like it was the middle of the night, he sounded like he'd run five miles and was getting ready to do ten more.

"What are you talking about?"

"Joey is giving the shoes to Charles. I heard him. On the phone."

"Where is he now?"

"He's asleep. I'm telling you—"

"What are you on?"

"It doesn't matter. I heard…"

"Eric. Go to sleep." The phone line went dead.

Eric hung up, squeezed the phone in his fist and silently screamed. Why wouldn't she listen to him? At the counter he chose two pink pills that looked like shrunken versions of the peppermints his grandfather used to suck on. They kind of smelled minty too, only much more pharmaceutical. He chewed them and went back to the couch. The calm overtook him within minutes and, by the time he fell asleep, he was as good as happy.

~~~~~

Kelly lay awake a long time wondering if she should call Eric back. Or call Joey. She shook her head and wished for someone, one person, she could really trust.

What Eric said didn't matter, he was paranoid and high. But she didn't know Joey as well as he did.

Eventually, she got up and dressed in jeans and a hoodie. In the hall closet she slipped on a pair of Jordana's winter gloves and found an empty shoebox. In the kitchen she grabbed two cotton dishtowels and a knife, then went to the garage.

Her car, backed into a parking spot between a Bronco and an old Ford pickup, was hidden enough to make her feel good about being able to remove the shoes without being seen. Her back was against a brick wall, so no one could sneak up from behind like Mark had. But she was also vulnerable. If he did show up, she wouldn't see him until he was directly in front of her car, and by then it would be too late to hide.

The backpack was still sitting on the plastic tarp in the trunk; she carefully opened it and pulled out the wrapped package. The knife easily cut through the tape and garbage bag, revealing a clear plastic box with a blue lid, the kind you can buy in the storage section of any store for a dollar. Inside were red shoes.

The lid opened with a *snap* that echoed throughout the garage.

Her breath caught.

They had deteriorated dramatically. The bottom of the box was littered with sequins and beads. One of the bows was falling off the side of the shoe and the "rubies" that were still attached to the middle of it were hanging by single threads. Many of the sequins had turned black around the edges or had large silver spots where the red paint had flaked off. The soles were peeling away from the bottom of the shoes. Gathered silk, the same black-brown color of old mud, was visible around the edges.

Carefully, using both hands, Kelly picked up one shoe, wrapped a dishtowel around it, and transferred it to the cardboard shoebox she'd brought from the house. When she tried to move the second shoe, its bow caught on the lip of the box and a large red bead fell with a hollow thud onto the plastic. Kelly tried to calm her shaking hands as she wrapped the shoe in the other dishtowel and set it inside the cardboard. She considered dumping the sequins and beads from the plastic box into the cardboard one, but decided against it. They would help prove the intentions of whoever ended up with the backpack.

She snapped the lid back on the plastic box and shoved it into the backpack with the ball of garbage bag and tape, and zipped the whole thing up. Then she used the tarp from the trunk to wrap the cardboard box and ran, with it, back to her apartment.

She wasn't sure yet exactly what she was going to do, but she needed to know whether she could really trust Joey before she gave him the shoes.

Y ou have them?" Joey met Kelly at her car in the library's deserted parking lot.

"Yes, they're in the trunk."

Joey nodded, circled to the back of the car, and waited.

"Where's Eric?"

"Sleeping it off."

"You took his car?"

Joey shrugged. "Couldn't wake him." He tapped on the trunk with his knuckles and she pulled the release, then stood next to him as he reached in and pulled out the banker's box. It was bigger than it needed to be, but all she could find to hold the backpack. She'd written the museum's address on it, then wrapped several layers of packing tape to prevent the lid from coming off without being cut through.

If Eric was right, and Joey was going to somehow get the package to Charles, she didn't know what would happen. If the box did end up with the cops, or the museum, she would get them the shoes too. Her plan involved framing Eric, and she felt guilty about it, but she had Jordana to consider. Plus, he claimed to have somehow been involved with the theft, so better he get punished for it than her.

She followed Joey around the side of the library, down to the path along the river. Steam was rising off the water, creating a miniature fog in the hazy dawn. He nestled the box in the shoreline brush a few dozen feet away from a huge culvert where old men stood to fish.

"What if it gets knocked into the river?" she asked.

"It won't." If it hadn't been for the shiny packing tape, the brown cardboard would have blended well with the undergrowth. Joey had covered it with leaves and branches, making it look as if it had been there a while, but still leaving it visible to an observant eye.

"You can take off," he said and began walking back to the parking lot. "Go to work. I'll hang here and see who takes it."

She tried to laugh. "I said I didn't want to leave the shoes with you, remember?"

Joey wheeled around, like he was going to come after her, but stopped himself. Kelly watched as his face went from angry to nonchalant. "You're not—you're leaving them along the river. Eric filled me in; I know how bad things are at ReEarth right now. I figured you had better things to do." He pulled a fishing pole and tackle box out of the back seat of Eric's car. "But suit yourself."

She looked at the river, and her car. "How long do you think it'll be before someone finds it?"

"Not sure. I'll call you."

She debated her options. She didn't trust him, and now that she'd seen that flash, she was scared. He reached an arm out and pulled her into a bear hug with her face buried in his bicep. It was just between being a show of power and a friendly send off. "Go," he said. "I've got this."

~~~~~

The streets were still deserted as she drove north past the police department and into the more residential area of Grand Rapids. She parked her car in front of a funeral home. There would be no reason for Mark or Joey to be in the area, and it was morbid, but if there was a visitation later her car would blend perfectly. If Eric did somehow get out later, he wouldn't see it either. He'd avoided the entire street ever since Brad's funeral. She wasn't sure why she felt she needed to hide from him too, but the realization came with an understanding of how alone she really was.

Maybe she should go to the police. How bad could it be? The statute of limitations was up. There had to be some way to prove she hadn't had the shoes the whole time. But they were so damaged. People would be mad and want someone to blame. And there was still Mark—Charles—to think about. What would he do if she showed up at the station with the shoes? She didn't think he'd thank her and go back to Chicago. She had to let Joey deal with that situation.

She called the office and lied about Jordana again.

"We really need you here," Ben said. "This is about to blow up. How is she doing? Do you know what it is?"

"Strep, I think." She picked it because it was contagious and already going around the office. "I'll do what I can to get there this afternoon."

"It's okay," Ben said quickly. "Do what you need to do. Take care of her and don't get sick yourself."

She promised she was on the verge of a plan and would be in touch soon, locked the car and began walking back to the library. She planned to keep an eye on the box, and Joey, through the wall of large windows facing the river. The chair she chose was hotel-lobby comfortable and hidden from the front of the library behind racks of books, but with an unobstructed view outside. She was worried that Joey and Mark/Charles may have already made the exchange, if that was what was really happening, but it only took a few seconds for her to spot the box in the brush and, a little way beyond it, Joey's dark blue shirt. His fishing pole flicked through the air as he cast and she let out a long breath. Eric was wrong about him.

She pulled her laptop out and started working, keeping one eye out the window. The latest note from

Joel was alarming. He agreed with her analysis of the new data, but said he wasn't convinced it completely refuted MfM's accusations. He was usually the one who refused to be convinced of anything, even their own research, so if he was finding validity in MfM's claims, their problems might be worse than she thought.

~~~~~

It took Eric a while to orient himself when he woke up, even though he was in his own apartment. The room seemed to tilt and straighten like a carnival ride. His mouth felt stuffed with cotton and his jaw ached.

Right away he noticed the chain was off the door, and the bedroom empty. The kitchen counter was cleared—no car keys, no candy bag, nothing. It already felt like he was walking in cement boots, the empty apartment made it worse.

It was too late to call Kelly. There was no point. He got a drink of water and went back to sleep.

~~~~~

The sun shining through the windows was warm and so bright Kelly had to squint to see her computer screen.

She hadn't slept at all, and her tired eyes could barely focus. She squeezed them shut and rubbed them with her knuckles.

A moment later, her phone began to ring, and she scrambled to silence it, but the librarian caught her eye and pointed to the sign on the doors. *Cell phone use allowed in lobby only!*

"I can't talk now," Kelly whispered.

The librarian glared.

"I need five minutes. It's important," Mira said.

"Okay, I—" In the corner of her vision Kelly saw the librarian start toward her. She quickly shoved her laptop into her bag and headed toward the lobby.

Mira had found a major hole in the MfM claims. It was exactly the break they'd all been looking for, but the call took almost twenty minutes. When Kelly got back to her seat, there was no sign of Joey, or the box.

Her phone buzzed and the librarian shot her another look. It was a text from Joey: *It's done.*

She hoped her smile looked apologetic as she rushed back out of the lobby with the phone to her ear. "Who took them?" she asked when Joey answered. "What time?"

"Happened about ten-thirty."

Basically, the same exact time Mira called.

"Some guy spotted it. He looked around a bit before he took it, but didn't try to get it open. He'll turn it in."

"How do you know?"

"Trust me. I know."

"Do you know who it was?"

"Nope."

"Then how will you know—"

"It's under control. Calm down."

Kelly let out a long breath and apologized. Joey promised to call if he heard anything. "And don't worry about Charles," he said. "That's taken care of."

She wanted to ask what he meant, but she didn't need to. If some random person had really found a box addressed to the museum outside of the library, they would have brought it inside. They wouldn't have taken it. If Charles was taken care of, it meant Eric was right. Joey had given him the package.

She waited another thirty minutes to be sure Joey was out of the area before beginning the uphill walk back to her car.

~~~~~

The next time Eric woke the sun was high in the sky and the television was on. He rubbed his face and saw Joey sitting in the chair, eating pizza.

"Sleeping beauty," Joey said. "Maybe next time don't steal from me, yeah?"

"You're my guest. I thought you bought them as a gift for my hospitality." Eric's thinking was clearer than it had been, but he was still sweaty and shaking as he went to the fridge. The twelve pack was gone. Even the bread he'd had on the counter was just an empty bag. "What the fuck, dude? Where is everything?"

"Kelly says she's worried about you. I think she's right. If you're sleeping entire days at a time, you need to get your shit together. I'm all about a little buzz, but you've got to be able to take care of business."

Eric wanted to cross the room and punch him in the face, but he didn't have the strength. Instead, he got a glass of water and ate a bowl of dry cereal.

Joey's phone rang. He glanced at the screen, up at Eric, then went into the bedroom and slammed the door.

Eric strained to hear, but could only make out a few words: "...find out...she's not that smart...take care of it...don't worry...handled..."

Joey was smiling when he came back to the living room. He fished in his pocket and pulled out the bag of pills, picked out three and handed them to Eric before sitting back down and picking up his pizza.

Eric looked from the pills to Joey. "Everything okay?"

"Yep," Joey said and took a huge bite. "Sorry I was being so rude."

~~~~~

Kelly had talked to Jordana on the phone, and the child was more than happy to get a second night at Sarah's.

At least she was safe. Kelly could feel the physical presence of the shoes in her closet the same way she had when they were in her car, but she tried to ignore it while she worked. Everyone was chasing Mira's lead.

Frank called. He'd seen Jordana and Sarah at Walmart. He told Kelly again he was worried about her and offered to help.

She was so close to telling him the truth. She could give him the shoes, he could say he was the one that found them, everything would be fine. Instead, she faked a dropped call. She couldn't pull him, or anyone else, into this mess.

It was going to cost her her job. She and Jordana were going to need to move again. Probably far away. But she couldn't think about any of that yet. Right now, she needed to focus. She had the solution for ReEarth's problem, and sent an email letting everyone know they needed a meeting at nine the next morning. She'd take care of this first, then the shoes.

It was only due to pure exhaustion that Kelly fell asleep at all.

~~~~~

She jolted awake with the first bang. Her neck hurt from the way her head had rested on the arm of the couch, but she didn't have any time to think about it.

"Kelly! Open up!" Joey yelled.

She ran to the door. As soon as she turned the knob he pushed his way through. "Where are the fucking shoes?"

She looked around for something to protect herself with, or words that would calm him. All she got was a squeaky noise that came out of the back of her throat.

He backed her against the wall and put a hand on either side of her head.

"I...I don't..." she tried to speak but couldn't.

"Don't fuck with me, Kelly. I don't have the patience."

"I didn't—" She stopped. Maybe it wasn't worth it. Maybe she should just give him the shoes and pretend she'd never had them. He wasn't going to take them to the cops. She wouldn't go to jail.

"The backpack had a box with some beads and sequins. That's it. No shoes."

She tilted her head down and looked at him through her eyelashes. If she was going to do this, she had to know for sure it would end this stupid charade. She and Jordana would be free, Eric would be free. She put her palm gently on Joey's chest. "Calm down," she said softly.

He cocked his head, and for a moment she thought he was trying to decide how hard to hit her. She braced herself. But instead of lifting his hand away from the wall, he softened his stance a little bit and she ducked out from underneath him.

"I'm sorry." The coo in her voice made her sick. She wasn't this person anymore. She couldn't believe she ever had been. "There must be something we can do."

He smiled and rested his hand on her hip. "I believe you. And I've already taken care of it. I got Charles a cashier's check this afternoon, and he's happily counting his money. But you got me into this mess. You're going to help me figure out how to get that money back."

She watched his eyes roam over her body and forced herself not to cringe or cross her arms while wishing she was wearing something else. The t-shirt and sweatpants were in no way sexy, but he seemed to like what he was seeing.

"We're either going to find those shoes, or you can earn the money back in other ways."

This was it. She would turn it all over to him. Once he saw how bad they were, he could decide whether to give them to Charles or burn them or sell them. She didn't care anymore. She batted her eyelashes and said, "What—"

A knock on the door followed by a frail wail stopped the words. "Kelly? Kelly? Kelly, I need your help."

She looked toward the sound of Mrs. McAlester's desperate voice. Joey backed up.

Kelly opened the door and found Mrs. McAlester slumped against the doorjamb, hugging her arm to her body. "Oh, Kelly, I'm so glad you're home. I think… I…" there were tears running down the old woman's face. "I think I dislocated my shoulder. Or something. I can't move my arm. It hurts so bad!"

"Okay, okay. Come here. Sit down." Kelly helped her to the kitchen table. "Should I call an ambulance?"

"Can you take me to the hospital? I can't afford…" her words were cut off by a fresh sob.

"I've got to get going," Joey said. Kelly was shoving ice into a plastic bag and Joey stepped up behind her, pinning her against the counter with his body. He leaned down so his mouth was right next to her ear. "We'll be in touch. Soon." He let a hand trail from her shoulder to her low back. It lingered there a moment, then he looked over at Mrs. McAlester. "I hope you feel better soon, ma'am."

Kelly didn't exhale until the door clicked shut behind Joey. She'd been so close. So stupidly close. Giving the shoes to Joey… First of all, she needed to turn them in, make right the fact that she hadn't done it when she had the chance originally. Second, if Joey really was working with Charles, why hadn't she even considered the consequences of the two of them *knowing* she'd lied? Stupid. It was just stupid.

Mrs. McAlester stood and the chair she'd been in scraped lightly on the floor, pulling Kelly back to reality and the ice. "Just let me get some shoes on and we'll head out."

Mrs. McAlester held up a finger, like she was listening for something. When they heard the outside door open and close she let her arm drop, and whispered, "Are you okay?"

Kelly blinked and grabbed for the older woman. "Be careful!"

Mrs. McAlester shooed her away with one hand and wiped the wetness away from her cheeks with the other. "I'm fine. I can cry on demand. Should have been an actress, shouldn't I?"

Kelly didn't know what to say.

"I saw him come in. I'm sorry. I'm not really this nosey…Oh, you know by now, yes, I am. I was up and I heard him and I thought you might need help. Are you okay?"

Kelly was shaking. The adrenaline had left and she couldn't help the tears that started in the corners of her eyes, then rushed in rivers down her cheeks.

Mrs. McAlester pulled her into a hug. "It's okay, honey. He's gone now." She looked around. "Where's Jordana?"

Kelly sniffled out that she was at a friend's, and Mrs. McAlester gently pulled her across the hall, into her apartment.

~~~~~

Kelly sat on the floral-print couch, wrapped in a hand-crocheted blanket, trying to stop the tears and the shaking. Mrs. McAlester was busy in the kitchen, heating water in a kettle and something else in the microwave. She set a warm cup of tea and a slice of bread and butter on the table beside the sofa.

Kelly shook her head, but Mrs. McAlester pushed the plate a little closer. "When was the last time you ate?"

Kelly took a long drink of the tea and a tiny bite of the toast. The warm liquid and the creamy butter mingled in her mouth and she chewed.

"Do you want to talk about it?"

She shook her head and took another bite. She was hungry.

"Are you safe?"

She didn't raise her eyes.

"Is Jordana safe?"

She looked up and nodded.

"Good. Did he hit you?"

She shook her head.

"How long have you been dating?"

"We're not."

Mrs. McAlester nodded. "Is that the problem? Is he pressuring you?"

Kelly almost laughed at "pressuring." She was so tired of lying and covering and trying to think of excuses, she just shook her head. "He helped Jordana's father steal the Ruby Slippers from that museum in Grand Rapids in oh-five."

Mrs. McAlester sat up. "Oh."

"And he thinks I know where they are."

"Do you?"

Kelly thought for a moment. She didn't know if it was the warm comfort of the apartment and the tea and toast, or if having come so close to telling Joey she just needed to get it out. Either way, she felt her head nodding.

Mrs. McAlester didn't say anything.

"But I didn't have anything to do with the theft. I just…" it sounded like a lie, and not even a good one, but she'd started, so she might as well finish. "I found them when we were setting up that mine over by Buhl—Whiteside? I guess Eric—that's the guy that was here that morning, with the banana bread?"

Mrs. McAlester nodded.

"His cousin found where Jared and Eric had hidden them initially and he moved them. Then he was killed and no one knew where they were."

"What are you going to do with them?"

Kelly shook her head. "I want to give them back. But everyone always thought I was involved. I can't…I don't…" she took a deep breath. "They're destroyed. I guess being out in the elements…I don't know. But if I turn them in everyone's going to assume that I've had them this whole time. I'm going to get arrested and I'm going to be blamed for not taking care of them. Honestly, I just don't care anymore. About any of it. But Jordana…"

Mrs. McAlester nodded.

Kelly stared into her tea cup.

"Well, nothing is ever solved in the middle of the night when you're too tired to think."

Kelly nodded and stood. "I need to go home—"

"Bullshit."

Kelly had never heard Mrs. McAlester so much as raise her voice, much less swear.

"You're going to sleep here. If that idiot comes back he'll think you're at the hospital with me."

"But what if he comes here?"

"I know his type. He's not coming back to check on an old lady. Come on. I've got an extra bedroom."

Mrs. McAlester walked Kelly down the apartment's short hall and left her at the door to a room with two twin beds decorated with stuffed animals. "This is where the grandkids sleep, but the mattresses are comfortable and the sheets are clean. There's extra blankets and pillows in the closet. Make yourself at home."

"I need my phone. In case Jordana calls."

Mrs. McAlester nodded. "Grab some clothes for tomorrow too. You don't need to go back there in the morning. Just in case."

Kelly went to her apartment and grabbed her laptop bag, a set of clothes, and her toothbrush. Back in Mrs. McAlester's apartment, she watched while the door was locked, deadbolted and chained, then let Mrs. McAlester pull her into another hug.

Eric lay awake a long time, his brain completely alert, but he couldn't get his body to move. He tried to remember the previous day, but all he could put together was the bowl of cereal, Joey offering three pills, and the word *cocktail*.

His cell phone was ringing, but he let it go to voicemail. When the call cleared he saw that it had been his mother, and that he'd missed four other calls from her. He hit the redial button.

"Oh, thank God!" she said.

He could tell she was crying, and fought to wake up and figure out what was going on.

"We thought you were dead!"

"What?"

"Your car...they found it... hit and run... destroyed..." the words were coming out between gasps as his mother calmed down.

He walked to the window and saw the empty spot where his car had been. He didn't have to check the bedroom to know Joey wasn't there. For one thing, there was no sound. But the keys were missing from the counter, and Joey's "generosity" only made sense if he was getting something in return. But if Eric's car was…then…

"Mom. I've got to go. I'll call you back."

"But—do you know who had your car?"

"I think so."

He hung up and dialed Joey's cell. It went straight to voicemail. There were two missed calls from Duluth numbers he didn't recognize, and one from the Grand Rapids Police Department. He turned on the TV and found the Duluth news.

There was a camera crew covering the story, and he identified the neighborhood right away. It was within blocks of Kelly's apartment. His car was barely recognizable, crushed under the front of a semi pulling an oil tanker. There were firefighters on the scene.

He turned the volume up, but caught only *"We'll be bringing you more developments as we have them,"* before the picture cut back to the studio and they switched to national news.

There was a knock on the door, and he did a quick sweep of the apartment. The gun…where?…In the car. Shit.

"Eric!" Detective Richards called.

Eric checked to be sure Richards was alone before he opened the door.

"We've been trying to call you," Richards said.

"I just woke up," Eric said. "My phone was on silent."

Richards nodded and noticed the TV. "You see the news?"

Eric nodded.

"It's your car."

He nodded again.

"Do you know who was driving it?"

Eric almost lied and said it was stolen, to put as much distance between himself and Joey as possible. But it didn't seem like it was worth the trouble. "Joey Ostberg."

Richards was making notes. "He from around here?"

"Used to be. His parents still live up by Chisholm. He was just in town visiting, though."

"You loaned him the car?"

Eric nodded.

Richards put a hand on his shoulder in what Eric was sure was probably supposed to be comfort, but it felt awkward, like he was going to spin him around and cuff him. "I'm sorry to tell you this, but if he was the driver, he didn't make it. We'll need to get a positive ID, of course, but it looks like the semi driver ran a light. He was crushed."

Eric nodded and fought the urge to sink into a chair.

"We need to get ahold of his next of kin. Do you have any idea how to contact them?"

Eric nodded and gave Richards Joey's parents' names. Richards thanked him, told him they'd be in touch, and left.

Eric called Kelly and listened to the phone ring. She didn't answer. He tried three more times then went to the shower.

~~~~~

The bed was small but comfortable. When she awoke in the morning, she could hear Mrs. McAlester moving around in the kitchen and the news on the TV. She checked her phone and saw three missed calls from Eric. Rather than listen to the messages, she called Jordana and promised to pick her up from school that afternoon. Then she thanked Elizabeth for their help and promised to return the favor.

In the bathroom, she washed her face and pulled her hair back into a bun.

"Did you sleep well?" Mrs. McAlester asked when Kelly entered the apartment's living area.

Kelly nodded. "I've got to get to work, though."

"Of course! Here's some breakfast. And coffee. You can bring the cup back later. If that guy shows up—"

"He won't," Kelly said. "He's more careful than that."

"Still. If he does, I'll call you. And the police."

"Thank you."

Mrs. McAlester pulled her into a hug. "It'll be okay."

Kelly nodded.

On the way to work, the middle of the night conversation came back to her. She wondered if it had been a dream, or if she really had told Mrs. McAlester she had the shoes. She couldn't have. She wouldn't have.

But if she had...she needed to move.

~~~~~

Kelly's legs felt weak as she walked into the office. The more she thought about it, the more she was sure she had told Mrs. McAlester everything. She knew the police were going to show up at some point during the day, and she wanted to put her head down on her desk and cry. Or sleep. Or cry until she fell asleep. But she was only one step off the elevator when Ben saw her.

He was getting coffee and, judging by the bags under his eyes, had gotten even less sleep than she had.

She took a deep breath and tried to switch into confident work mode. "We're meeting at nine," she said. "I need everyone."

He nodded. "Should we talk first?"

She shook her head and kept walking. "I've got a few things to get ready. Don't worry. It'll be fine."

"Kelly?"

She turned. "Yeah?" Out of the corner of her eye she saw Frank approaching from the hallway.

"I appreciate all you've done," Ben said. "Especially with Jordana sick. I don't take it lightly that you've kept going on all of this while trying to take care of her. Thank you."

Kelly nodded and walked as quickly as she could without making eye contact with anyone, but when she turned to close her office door, Frank was there.

"Did you hear the sirens last night?"

"What?"

"The sirens. There was a huge accident—didn't you see it? Which way do you drive to work?"

She told him her route and he nodded. "Yeah, you wouldn't have seen it then. But I'm surprised you didn't hear them. You must be a heavy sleeper. Pull your computer out."

She set the laptop up on the desk and he pulled up the local news channel's website. "Check it out."

Even with the front completely gone Kelly recognized the car. She gasped, swallowed, and gasped again.

"Are you okay?"

She shook her head. "I have to make a phone call."

She took deep breaths to try to keep from panicking while she looked at her cell phone. The time of the calls…she read the time of the accident. The calls came after. But…

Her finger hovered over Eric's name in her call log, but before she got the courage to press the button her phone began ringing in her hand, startling her so much she dropped it on the floor. She saw his name and snatched it off the carpet. "Hello?"

"Kelly!" Eric sounded relieved.

She felt tears starting in the corners of her eyes. "You're okay?"

"Yeah, I am."

"The car—" She refused to let herself cry. He was okay. She had to run the meeting, then she'd get out of there.

"It wasn't me."

"What?"

"It wasn't me. Joey took my car."

"I don't—"

"Kelly. Joey's dead."

She sank down in her seat. "But—"

"They said the truck was stolen from that gas station down the street. The driver ran away on foot. No one can find any sign of him."

~~~~~

Kelly's fingers shook as she passed the packets of information around the conference room. She tried to keep her voice steady, but it wasn't working. Frank was watching her. He knew something was up. She hoped everyone else would think it was the same exhaustion they were feeling and not ask her any questions.

"Mira gets credit for the discovery," she said while everyone was reading. "And the next week is crucial." She turned to Nicole. "How soon can we get a spot on the local news?"

"Normally, two days. But with this, we might be able to push it up."

Kelly nodded. "Two days is good. That'll give us time to get everything in writing, in layman's terms. We can do a blitz then, hit the newspapers and the television all the same day. I also want to give Minnesotan's for Minerals a chance to recall their stance on their own. I think it'll look better coming from them first. If they'll do it."

Kelly looked to Ben, then at everyone else in the room. "Any questions?"

Frank raised his hand. Kelly flinched and braced herself. "Yes?"

"How are we rewarding Mira? We all owe her our jobs, don't we?"

Mira smiled and blushed. Ben said, "That's to-be-determined, but we'll figure something out. A cake? A bouquet of flowers? Big fat bonus?"

Everyone laughed.

"We're not out of the woods yet," Kelly said. "There's still work to do. Assignments are on the final page of your packet. See me or Mira if you have questions."

~~~~~

Back in her office, she closed the door, sat down, and tried to decide what to do. She could get Jordana from school, right then, and leave town. She had some money in savings. But she didn't know where they'd go.

Her phone was flashing, Mark's number showing on her missed calls list. She braced herself, pushed the button and held the phone to her ear. She wasn't breathing and could feel herself getting light headed when his voice broke through.

"Kelly, I'm sorry I didn't get to do this in person. I'm sure you've seen my email by now, but wanted to thank you again for your help. I'm still working on the case, so if you do think of anything else, please give me a call. Hopefully I'll see you again soon."

Email? Kelly scanned through her inbox and didn't see anything from him. She flipped over to her personal email, which she hadn't checked for days, since usually all she got was ads and SPAM.

The message had come in at six-fifty-three the night before.

Kelly,

Something has come up in Chicago and I need to go back to deal with it. I've very much enjoyed working with you. I'm still determined to find those shoes, and if you think of any other information about Jared that would help, I would appreciate you getting a hold of me. But, even if there isn't any new information, I would love to stay in touch. You have my contact information and I have yours.

Best,

Mark

She sat back in her chair. He was gone? Just like that?

She called Eric and read him the email. "I don't think he was Charles," Kelly said. "If he was, why would he up and leave?" She was replaying what Joey had told her the night before about paying him, but Joey was still convinced Kelly had the shoes. If this guy was everything Eric and Joey had made him out to be, no amount of money would make him disappear.

"He is," Eric said. "It's a ploy. I'm telling you— I've got to go. Joey's mom is ringing."

"I'm sorry."

"Yeah. Me too."

~~~~~

The next week was a blur. Kelly had a meeting with the main guy from MfM and he'd held a press conference the same day saying they were retracting their earlier data. They were still against the mines, though. They believed the industry was inherently unsafe and unsustainable, and they would be re-conducting their tests.

Although Senator Burdock hadn't announced a new official position on the mines, he had voted to approve a lifting of the temporary injunction and work had begun at Grace again.

Mrs. McAlester never said anything about the shoes other than, "Sometimes, when we're tired and scared, we say things. No one should ever hold that against us."

Joey's funeral was in Chisholm. There was no visitation, no wake. There was no body. At the ceremony there was an urn on the altar next to a picture of Joey in a suit. Kelly hugged his parents and offered her condolences.

The news outlets that had reported so heavily on Mark's involvement in the investigation didn't say anything about him leaving town, a point Eric made every chance he got. He said he couldn't let her "drift back into her comfortable oblivion" and didn't know what to do other than persistently remind her of the truth: Mark was Charles. Charles had killed Jared, Brad and, now, Joey. He was coming back for them.

She agreed, it was suspicious that they hadn't mentioned it, but she argued: if Mark really was Charles, and he'd killed for the shoes, why would he just give up now and go back to Chicago? It made as little sense as Charles showing up after all these years.

~~~~~

One morning, an hour after he'd tried to call Kelly and make her understand about Charles, Dale showed up at Eric's apartment with boxes. Apparently Kelly had called Sherrie, and Sherrie had called his parents. Dale told Eric he had made an appointment with a psychiatrist and that Eric could choose between moving back into their house or going to rehab.

It didn't take long to pack, and Eric didn't feel any type of nostalgia as he dropped his keys into the box outside of the building manager's office.

Exactly a month after Joey died, Ben woke Kelly up with a phone call seven minutes before her alarm was scheduled to go off.

"What do you mean?" she asked. He'd already explained it twice, but the sleep fog in her head was keeping her from fully understanding.

Ben's voice was scratchy and distorted, she couldn't tell how much of it was from the cold he'd been battling and how much was due to crappy cell service.

"How much damage?"

She couldn't hear his answer, and then the sound cut out completely. She pushed a button to end the call and texted *I'm on my way*.

While she pulled on jeans, she called Mrs. McAlester, then layered a hoodie over a long sleeve t-shirt, and grabbed wool socks for inside her boots.

"Jordana?" Kelly pushed the bedroom door open, remembered, and knocked lightly. The child was all about privacy these days, and had invoked a "No entering without permission" rule that, no matter how she tried, Kelly kept forgetting. It was hard to believe that someone so young could be so independent. Jordana didn't answer, so Kelly flipped on the light, and flopped down on the bed with her head on Jordana's shoulder.

"Oh my gosh! Sleeping Beauty!" Kelly's voice was fake sing-song and she saw Jordana smile before turning her head the other way.

"My darling! How will we ever go on without you?"

"Shut up, Mom!" Jordana tried to roll away and pull her blanket over her head, but Kelly was holding it down.

"Get up!" Kelly patted the lump that was Jordana's shoulder. I've got to go to work. Right now."

"M-o-o-o-o-m. What time is it?"

"Six thirty. Mrs. McAlester is coming over."

"I can sleep for another hour!"

"But if I let you do that, you might sleep for two, three, maybe even four more hours. Who knows? The sky's the limit. It's my job, as a mother, to be sure you are sleep deprived but at school. Get up."

Jordana groaned. "Leave me alone!"

"Plus, if I left, Mrs. McAlester would get all the pleasure of waking you. And I can't start my day without the extra love."

Jordana could never go back to sleep once she'd been awakened—it was a huge problem when she was a baby—so Kelly was safe to finish getting ready.

When she got to the kitchen, Jordana was at the table with a bowl of cereal and Mrs. McAlester had started a pot of coffee. A sweet, homey smell was coming from the oven. "Do you have time to wait? I whipped up some cinnamon rolls!"

Kelly smiled and shook her head while she filled her coffee thermos. "No. But thank you. I'm sorry it's so early."

Mrs. McAlester made a dismissive noise with her lips and waved at Kelly. "You know I've been up for almost two hours. I'm sorry I didn't have something ready to go for your breakfast."

"It's okay. I'll eat hers," Jordana said, obviously no longer mad about the missed sleep.

Kelly hugged Mrs. McAlester, then went around the table and kissed Jordana's head. "Have a good day. Love you."

"Love you too, Mom!"

~~~~~

At Grace, it was hard to tell anything was wrong, except for the fact that no one was working and the single word painted on the entrance to the building: *Die*.

Ben met her at her car.

"How bad is it?" She got out, but at the last second reached back in for her coffee cup.

"Dirt in the gas tanks, they're going to need to be entirely replaced. The wires—all of the electronics are destroyed."

"Any idea who did it?"

Ben shook his head. "Someone who was mad about work starting again. I've already called the guy from MfM. He says they had nothing to do with it."

Kelly nodded. "Of course he does."

"There's going to be a press conference here at three. Can you stay for it?"

Kelly agreed. Frank and Jim pulled up together a moment later.

"Shitty way to end your career," Ben said, shaking Frank's hand.

Frank shrugged. "I can stay on if you want me to. But Jim's got everything covered."

Kelly had completely forgotten this was Frank's last week.

She watched Frank as he and Jim toured the destruction together, the way he explained things and answered Jim's questions. The damage was almost all exclusively to heavy equipment; it didn't appear anyone had gotten inside any of the buildings, or the mine shaft itself. He was patient, thorough, and confident. Again, she wondered if he might be able to help with the shoes.

He turned, as if he knew she was thinking about him. She opened her mouth to ask if she could speak with him in private, but, before she could say anything, her phone rang. She looked, saw Eric's name, and hit the silence button.

"You can get it," Ben said. "There's really nothing for us to do here."

Kelly nodded but hit ignore. She didn't want to talk to Eric.

It started buzzing again immediately.

"Go ahead," Frank said.

She put the phone to her ear and walked toward her car. "This isn't a good time."

"You at Grace? Charles did it. You know that, right? It was him, sending us a message."

"Eric, calm down. Charles is gone. If there ever was a Charles. I'm starting to think he was someone you and Joey made up to scare me." It was actually a thought she'd had a few times, but never really acknowledged. She surprised herself by vocalizing it.

Eric shouted at her. "McDonald was Charles! Why don't you understand that? Why don't you understand how much trouble you're in?"

Frank approached her. "Is everything okay?" he whispered.

She nodded, held up a finger, and said, "Eric, I've got to go."

~~~~~

Eric slammed the phone down. He couldn't do it anymore. If she wasn't going to listen to him, that was one thing. But to accuse him of lying…all he'd ever done is try to protect her.

Things had actually been better. The new doctor had changed his medication and he was sleeping. Between that, and the fact that his parents were making him take home drug tests, he had cut back on the self-medicating. Stevens' Landscaping was in its normal seasonal lull—waiting for the snow removal portion of the business to ramp up. He'd been working closely with his father to create and implement an exit plan where Dale would truly retire. He'd turn over control of the company to Eric on January first and only come in to visit. The hardest thing Eric had to do was gain the trust of the employees, and he was doing his best. He showed up early, stayed late, and worked hard.

But he still had the nightmares. And he was sure he'd seen Charles following him in Walmart one day. He'd dropped his basket and sprinted out of the store. In the parking lot he turned and saw he was alone, save for plain-clothes security that had followed him out. Eric had obediently emptied his pockets, made up a story about hearing his car alarm, and went back inside to finish shopping.

He knew the mine damage was a message from Charles.

The vandalism wasn't the work of environmentalists, or Charles. It was a drunk ex ReEarth employee, trying to get revenge after he'd been fired for missing too many days of work. He might have gotten away with it, too, had he not bragged about it on the internet.

Kelly did a round of interviews discussing the environmental impact of the mine, and a public debate between her and one of the geologists from MfM was covered by the national news networks. Besides the fact that she was more personable and compelling than the guy from MfM, her data was better. There was no argument over who won the debate, and the permits they'd been waiting on for months began rolling in.

The only thing she had hanging over her head were the shoes, still in the cardboard box in her closet. She couldn't give them back, probably ever, without minimally drawing suspicion. And she didn't think Mark was who Eric and Joey accused him of being, but it wasn't worth the risk to find out.

She couldn't bring herself to burn them, or toss them in Lake Superior, either. She still couldn't stand to see them destroyed.

~~~~~

Weeks went by, and Eric kept catching glimpses, but didn't see any real sign of Charles. His doctor listened patiently when he talked about the nightmares, thinking he was seeing his shooter in public places, then increased Eric's anxiety medication and upped his counseling sessions to twice a week.

It helped. The medicine made him tired, and he had to fight to make it through each day, but he was doing good work. He was no longer seeing Charles anywhere, the dreams were less frequent.

Sherrie started bringing Matt over for longer visits, and even agreed to let the boy go with Eric and Dale to a hunting expo in Duluth the week before Halloween. He called and asked Kelly if she wanted to get the kids together, maybe at Chuck E. Cheese's, but she declined.

~~~~~

Eric was out quoting a landscaping contract for a new condo complex when a truck with tinted windows rolled slowly by. He couldn't see inside, and tried to ignore it as he talked to the developer. But it came back and he thought he saw someone waving. On the third pass, he saw through the windshield. Charles's smile was huge. He gave Eric a thumbs-up before gunning it and driving away.

"Did you see that?" he asked the developer.

"Probably just looking." The developer pointed at a *For Sale* sign in the yard across the street. "I hope he buys it. It's been for sale for too long."

But the next week, at the gun show, Eric saw him again. Matt and Dale were taking a break, eating hotdogs at a picnic table near the perimeter of the civic center while Eric browsed. He came around a corner and saw Charles holding a small revolver, talking to one of the vendors. Eric watched as Charles handed over a roll of bills, the vendor counted them, then pulled a small lock box from under the table. Charles put the gun in, flipped the latch shut, looked up and waved, as if he knew Eric was there the whole time. Charles reached his hand up and waved.

It wasn't a hallucination. The vendor also looked over and gestured for him to come see the table. He tried to act like he hadn't seen them, turned, walked as calmly as he could through the crowd, and ran out the emergency exit.

He was at the car before he remembered his father and son. He called Dale, told him he was sick, and they needed to leave. By the time they got to the car Eric was shaking and sweating. Dale told Matt not to worry, it was probably food poisoning, and let the kid sit in the front all the way back to Grand Rapids while Eric lay across the back seat.

~~~~~

Dale dropped Matt at Sherrie's then took Eric to the emergency room. "There is something wrong with my son. I think he overdosed. We need a drug test," he told the receptionist.

"It's...not..." Eric tried to speak but his teeth were chattering. It was a panic attack. He had medication at home he could take, but didn't have the strength to argue with his father.

A nurse wheeled him into an exam room and took his vitals, then inserted a needle into his arm and took a few vials of blood. "The doctor will be in in a moment."

A few hours later Eric was released. Dale agreed not to tell his mom about it—they didn't want to worry her—and apologized for not believing when Eric had told him he wasn't using drugs. They'd given him a saline IV and he'd calmed down enough on his own to prove it was a simple panic attack. He wanted to call and warn Kelly about Charles, but she wouldn't have believed him anyway.

Hunting was supposed to be good for him. Cathartic. He'd spent every November since he was twelve in the woods, and his doctor stressed the importance of maintaining a routine.

Eric had told him how seeing Charles at the gun show had triggered the panic attack, but the doctor didn't seem concerned. "Post-traumatic stress is never gone. We only learn to control it," he'd said. He'd added something about the shooter still being in jail, and Eric hadn't argued.

The drive to his grandparents' old property was bringing back bad memories. He'd talked to the therapist about the possibility of this happening, and they'd planned out a series of breathing exercises. Eric used the first as he passed the access road to Grace. He parked a few miles further down the highway, as close as he could get to his deer stand, and sat for a moment, letting the memories come. Holidays at his grandparents' house, running through the woods with Brad and Kelly, helping Jared hide the shoes. How Brad had followed them and been such a dick, but given them a ride back to the car when he realized Jared's ankle was broken.

The cold morning air rushed in when he opened the door and pulled his gun, legally traveling inside its case with the ammunition separate, out of the back seat of the truck he'd bought with his insurance settlement. He filled the pockets of his blaze-orange jacket with shells and stared into the woods, trying to see the stand he'd built with his dad so many years earlier.

There was more traffic on the highway than he was used to, and he had to actively tell himself to stop looking at all of the drivers, trying to see if one of them was Charles. He hadn't seen any sign of him since that day in Duluth, and was almost convinced that hadn't really happened either. As he waited for an opening to cross the street, a pickup that he recognized from the drive up approached. The custom pinstripe down the side caught Eric's eye again: light blue faded into yellow and exploded into fireworks over the gas tank. If someone had explained it to him, he would have said it sounded stupid. But it actually looked really cool.

At the last second he looked into the driver's window. His heart stopped. Charles smiled and waved. There was no question it was him. Except…it couldn't be. The truck had been going at least sixty miles an hour. There was no way Eric could have actually gotten a clear view of the driver, much less had eye contact with him.

He shook his head, took a deep breath, and crossed the road. Within a few minutes he was deep into the white and brown trunks of birch and maple trees, crunching on leaves that had fallen but not yet lost all their color. Even covered with frost the yellows, oranges and occasional red would jump out at him as he looked for signs of wildlife.

As a kid he'd trudged through snow, sometimes as deep as his knees, while hunting. He'd hated it, but the white ground made tracking much easier than a carpet of leaves. There were signs of deer everywhere, and by the time he got to the stand he wasn't thinking about anything but finding and shooting one of the bucks that had been rubbing their antlers all over the trees.

He hung his gun over his shoulder and climbed carefully up to the stand, the rungs of the nailed-to-the-tree ladder in less than perfect condition. The stand itself, made of old two-by-fours left over from one of his grandfather's projects, was as solid as ever. Eric settled onto the little bench, leaned his back against the trunk, and pulled out an energy bar.

All around him was silence, and noise. The squirrels talked to each other and ran through the thinning canopy, stockpiling for the winter that could start any day. The trees creaked like old buildings, their branches rubbed together and leaves tumbled in the wind.

A stick snapped and Eric's eyes jerked toward the sound. He almost laughed. Wild turkeys. Three of the fat brown birds wandered slowly through, pecking now and again at the ground, their wattles wiggling back and forth. He would have shot one for Thanksgiving dinner, but he didn't have the right gun, or the required permit, and, if he shot, he'd scare away any deer in the area. Instead, he watched them and tried to tune his ears to hear around their movements.

The flash of blue he saw at first could have been anything. A weird bend of the trees and a glimpse of the sky. A blue jay that was late flying south. The black feathers of a crow reflecting the sun. But the second time, it was closer. His hands tensed on his gun. One of the turkeys started talking and Eric glanced at it. When he looked back, there was nothing. He wondered if he'd seen anything at all, or if it was another hallucination.

It couldn't have been another person; anyone in the woods this time of the year wore blaze orange. Even if they weren't head to toe, they had it on somewhere. When he was a kid, his grandmother had made him wear an orange cap to play in her yard from October until Thanksgiving. "Never can be too careful," she always said.

The turkeys eventually moved on and the woods' silence settled around Eric again. He heard another stick break, saw another flash of blue, and raised the gun to look through the scope. There was no round in the chamber, so he felt only a mild twinge of guilt for pointing where he wasn't planning to shoot.

It took a few seconds to orient himself in the scope's zoom, and even longer to see anything other than naked trees. First, he found the turkeys, still slowly moving away. Another stick broke and he swung the gun a few degrees north and caught another hint of blue. He focused in and saw a hooded sweatshirt, square jaw, binoculars, and hat.

Charles raised his hand and waved. "Hey, Eric, how's it going?"

Eric stared at him through the scope and felt his heart beating against the back of his ribs. He tried to remember to breathe. He couldn't lose it now.

"I'm not going to hurt you. Put the gun down, okay?"

Eric shook his head and the gun mimicked his movement.

"I'm not here for you. I want the shoes. Give them to me."

"I don't have them."

"What? I didn't hear you. Put the gun down."

The gun came away from his face. "I don't have the fucking shoes!" Eric screamed.

"Come on now. There's no reason to freak out. I know you have them. You've always had them. I want them."

"Why can't you let it go? You've been paid. Twice. Just let it go."

Charles laughed without smiling. "Yeah. Joey. That guy. He thought it was all about the money. It was for a while. See, when this all started, I didn't give a shit about the actual shoes. Really, I still don't. I just *want* them. Besides," he chuckled again, "I don't think Joey's going to pay me again, and you and Kelly sure as hell don't have any money."

"Leave her alone!"

The sound of the turkeys, now behind Eric, talking again, blended with Charles's chuckle.

"Yeah, she was his soft spot too. Both of them, really. What'd that girl do for all of you?"

"Fuck you," Eric spat. "She's a good person."

"Good at something!"

Eric raised the gun and looked at Charles through the scope. He was smiling, a wad of tobacco pushing out his lower lip. He raised his hands and turned his head slightly as he spat. "Put the gun down, Eric."

"What are you going to do with them? Even if we could find them, they're probably trash."

"Maybe, maybe not. Maybe I'll turn them in for the reward. Maybe I'll sell them myself. Maybe I'll restore them and become a national hero."

A snort, somewhere between a laugh and a cough, came out of Eric's throat. He lowered the gun.

"I thought you said this wasn't about the money."

Charles shrugged and spit again. There was no sign of any emotion from him at all, not even hate or disdain. He was like a preprogrammed robot that couldn't respond to outside stimuli.

"None of it matters. If you wanted them so bad, maybe you should have asked Brad where he put them before you shot him. We don't have the shoes." Eric hated that his voice was trembling. He couldn't tell whether Charles believed him or not.

"Maybe you do, maybe you don't. But I've been fucked over by the whole situation too many times. If you don't have them now, you're going to find them. Actually, Kelly. Kelly's going to find them. Because she's got the most to lose. She's got the motivation."

Charles's hand went into the pocket of his sweatshirt and Eric saw black metal. He didn't think as he chambered a round and raised the scope to his eye, and he didn't feel the steel trigger under his finger until his shoulder absorbed the recoil.

~~~~~

"I need your help."

"Eric, I'm at work," Kelly was holding the phone between her shoulder and ear, typing on the computer with one hand while flipping through a small stack of papers with the other. She found the page she was looking for, squinted to read the print more clearly, and typed quickly with both hands. "What's wrong?"

"Kelly. I need your help. Right now."

She stopped typing and sat up, holding the phone in her hand now. She could hear his teeth chattering.

"RIGHT NOW!" he screamed.

"Calm down." She was trying to use her "mom" voice without sounding condescending. "Where are you?"

"I'm...I'm..."

"Are you safe?"

"I don't know." Something in his voice was breaking. "I think so."

"Tell me where you are. I'll call your dad."

"No. I need you. Now."

"What about Sherrie? Can I call her? Where are you?" Mira walked in, her tablet extended like she wanted Kelly to read something on it, but Kelly held up her hand, shook her head, and Mira retreated, closing the door behind her. The door to the lab was still open, but there was no one in there.

"He's dead."

Kelly stood. "Who's dead? Where are you? What happened?"

It took Eric nearly a minute to stammer out the name. "Charles."

She unplugged her computer and shoved it, its cords, and the stack of papers she'd been flipping through into her bag. Her jacket was hanging on the back of her door, she grabbed it but didn't put it on. "Hang on," she said into the phone. She stopped at Mira's desk. "I have an emergency. Email whatever you were going to show me. I'll get back to you as soon as possible."

"Do you want me to tell—"

Kelly didn't stay to listen to the question, she was already out the door and on the stairs. She couldn't wait for the elevator. "Eric. Tell me where you are."

"I'm out by Grandpa's. I went hunting. He was there and…I didn't think…"

"Stay put. I'm on my way."

~~~~~

She should have kept Eric on the phone, kept him calm. But she couldn't because she wasn't calm herself. Jordana had volleyball practice, so Kelly had a little extra time before she needed to pick her up, but there was no way she could get to Chisholm and back in time. She called Elizabeth and asked if Jordana could spend the night.

"That would be great! We can take her to the tournament tomorrow too, if you want to meet us there later."

The volleyball tournament. She couldn't miss it. Jordana had been talking about it for two weeks, but still Kelly had completely forgotten. "Yeah, that would be great. Thank you." She was careful to keep her eyes on the road, stay within seven miles an hour of the speed limit, and not cut anyone off as she wove through Friday afternoon traffic. She called and had Jordana pulled out of class to tell her the plan. By then, she was out of town and driving past the nearly-naked trees that lined the highway. A few weeks before, she and Jordana had driven up the north shore and hiked near Grand Marais to enjoy the final burst of fall color. Jordana was getting into photography and had captured some beautiful shots of the leaves, waterfalls, and lakes that day. She had been talking about trying to get some wildlife photographs by going "hunting" with a camera instead of a gun. Kelly had actually considered asking Eric to take her. Stupid.

~~~~~

Eric put his gun on the floorboard in the back of the truck and analyzed his options.

He could plead accident. Charles was in the woods without orange on. It was a hunting hazard, and, unfortunately, happened every year. Except everyone knew that "Mark" had been looking into the theft, and that Eric and Jared had been friends. It was going to get an extra look, someone was going to say he shot him over the investigation.

Eric's hands were shaking. The anxiety pills his doctor had prescribed weren't doing anything. He was sitting behind the steering wheel, but couldn't seem to get the key in the ignition to drive away. If he left the body, maybe animals would find it before the cops did.

It was still a risk.

He reached under his seat. The zippered bag he'd stashed had two large white pills that looked like Tylenol. Eric put both in his mouth, chewed until they were a disgusting acid-y pulp, and swallowed. Then he began walking through the woods toward his grandparents' house.

~~~~~

The drive took too long. She set the cruise to keep from going as fast as she wanted to. Getting stopped would be bad. Especially if…There was no way Eric was telling the truth. It was another hallucination. It had to be. Charles, if he'd ever really existed, was gone. Eric couldn't have killed him.

Eric wouldn't kill anyone.

She tried to call him back but got his voicemail and prayed he was planning on meeting her at his grandparents' old house. What if she couldn't find him?

What if she did, and it was true? What if he was sitting there with a body?

She shook her head and wondered if she should call someone for help—his parents, her parents, Sherrie, maybe even Detective Richards or Frank—but something kept her from picking up the phone.

~~~~~

The house was empty, he knew, so he didn't even look there. He'd helped clear it out. In the garages, all of the tools had been removed, but there were still piles of scrap wood and metal, broken appliances, engine parts, stuff that needed to be hauled to the landfill but no one had ever done it.

He surveyed the options and remembered what his dad had suggested when they'd signed the paperwork to hand the homestead over to ReEarth. "If I were them, I'd burn all the barns to the ground. They're not stable, they're liable to blow over or incinerate during a good lightning storm."

Burning the barns down would do nothing but make Charles's body more likely to be found.

But burning the body…

He checked his phone and saw that Kelly had called back but hadn't left a message. It didn't matter now, though. He was going to take care of it himself.

Lighting the body where it fell, in the woods full of dead and drying leaves, would very likely bring out the fire department before enough of Charles had been destroyed. The only option was to get him back here and make it look like a bonfire. Get it hot enough to destroy all evidence, then pile so much wood on top that no one would ever dig through.

Even if someone saw a trail of blood through the woods, no one would care. It was hunting season, someone was probably dragging a deer out every other day.

In the scrap heap Eric found a tarp and a slab of plywood that was big enough to hold the body. There was a lone bungee cord hanging from the wall, left there to hold the door open. Eric grabbed it too, and carried everything back to Charles's body.

The shot had gone directly through Charles's eye and Eric had to avoid looking at the face in order to work without throwing up. The pistol had fallen next to the body and confirmed what Eric already knew: he'd had no choice. Charles would have killed him. His hands trembled as he draped the tarp over the body, gathered the bloody leaves under Charles's head, and rolled it all onto the plywood. He strapped it down with the bungee cord and started pulling.

He was tired and sweaty by the time he got out of the woods, but had solidified his plan.

In the garage, he found an engine that still had some gas in it and emptied it over the make-shift sled. He used his lighter to ignite a pile of dead leaves on the body, then once it was fully engulfed, he carefully began covering it with scrap wood, making sure not to add it too fast for the fire to grab each new piece. When the pile got to chest height, he began banking it, tee-pee style, funneling the smoke straight up in the air. From the highway it wouldn't look any different than any of the other chimney trails in the night sky.

~~~~~

Kelly had visited the house and garages one time since ReEarth bought the property, on a tour, and had gotten such an eerie feeling she'd avoided it completely ever since.

255

Even with her brights on, the headlights weren't penetrating more than a few feet in front of the vehicle as she bounced along the overgrown driveway. Finally, the tree line broke. From the clearing, she could see a fire, nearly twenty feet tall, burning too close to the old barn. The tops of the flames licked at the trees above, large pieces of smoldering ash floated in the air like lightning bugs.

Eric's face was in a shadow, but she could see the glow of his eyes. He was holding something that looked like a gun, it took a minute for her to realize it was a bent stick. She took a deep breath and a step toward him, keys in her hand, without closing the door or shutting off the car's lights. It didn't appear he'd seen her pull up, so she called to him, afraid of what might happen if he was startled. "Eric?"

He turned and lifted his hand to wave. She took a step back and he dropped the stick. "Sorry. I didn't mean to freak you out earlier."

She relaxed a little and began walking toward him, but her heels kept sinking, too high and too narrow for the thick grass.

"He's in there," Eric said.

His voice was completely calm. Normal Eric. She couldn't remember the last time he'd sounded so natural.

"It was the only way I could...you know..."

Kelly looked through the flames but could only make out what looked like old pallets, stacked several feet high, in the middle of a tee pee of scrap wood. She opened her mouth, tried to think of what to say, but nothing came out.

"We're safe now. I didn't think I had it in me. I always thought to myself...what would I do if I met him alone again? He tried to talk to me, told me he wasn't dangerous. But I wasn't that stupid. I didn't trust him. And I was right. He would have shot me and left me out here to rot. If he was here to talk, why did he follow me? Why'd he have a gun?"

Kelly half-listened as Eric's babbling became less and less coherent. He talked about the mine and Brad and Jared and the shoes and Charles and Mark and the cops that wouldn't believe him and Joey giving him pills and telling him not to worry and how no one was safe before but now they were, he'd made them safe.

"Where's your truck?" Kelly asked when he'd gotten quiet.

He pointed through the woods. "Way over there."

He raised his arm, like he was going to maybe hug her, and she subtly took a step to the side, out of his reach. The arm dropped as though it had forgotten why it was there in the first place.

He cocked his head. "Do you have anything to drink? I'm thirsty."

She shook her head.

He shrugged and turned back to the fire.

"What do you want to do?" she asked.

"Can you give me a ride back to my truck?"

"Should you drive?"

"Yeah, I suppose."

"Suppose what?"

He looked at the fire for a long moment, then at her, a sheepish smile on his sweat and ash streaked face. Then he turned and stumbled down the hill. Kelly watched but couldn't make her feet move until he was standing at the passenger door.

~~~~~

He smelled sweet and sweaty and musty all at the same time. Gasoline, smoke and dirt competed for recognition inside her nose. She rolled the windows down and made her way slowly out of the driveway. She wasn't very good at driving in reverse under normal circumstances. Backing around trees and ruts in the dark was nearly impossible, but, with the fire, there was no room to turn around. Eventually, she made it to the highway and was thankful there were no other cars on the road.

She was worried about where to take him, how to convince him not to drive, but Eric fell asleep almost immediately and barely woke twenty minutes later when she helped him into the back seat of his truck. She fished the keys out of his pocket and tossed them in the truck's bed. If a cop came by, he could prove he had no intention of driving.

She locked the doors, cracked the windows, and breathed a silent prayer of thanks for the warm night.

~~~~~

The drive back to Duluth seemed to take a lot longer than the drive out to Chisholm had. By the time she pulled into the apartment's garage, the whole thing felt like a dream. Eric hadn't really killed anyone. He'd drunk too much and had a bonfire on his grandparents' old property. It didn't matter she hadn't seen any alcohol. Maybe he'd taken something. His gun was in his truck. He probably wasn't even hunting.

The semis on the highway, passing so closely his truck rocked back and forth, woke him while the sun was just starting to lighten the sky. He stretched, checked his phone and saw three missed calls from his parents and a text from Kelly.

Ur keys r n back

He looked out the window and saw them there, lying in the bed for anyone in the world to grab. His shoulder was still sore from the recoil, but the panic he was so used to constantly running through his head was gone. No one was after him anymore. It was over. His mind was completely still.

He tipped one of his anxiety pills into his hand and flipped it into his mouth because he was supposed to take it in the morning, not because he needed it.

Had he looked, he would have seen the gray curls of smoke still reaching above the trees near his grandparents' house as he pulled away. But he didn't. He didn't even look in the rearview mirror.

~~~~~

Kelly didn't dream that night but slept more soundly than she had in years and pushed away all thoughts of Eric when she woke up in the morning and dressed in the team sweatshirt with jeans. On the way to the gym she stopped and bought two dozen of Jordana's favorite doughnuts for the team and single cups of coffee for herself, Elizabeth, and the coaches. She would have bought a big to-go container for all the parents to share, but didn't have time to wait for it to be brewed. They would understand.

The girls played great and Kelly enjoyed finally spending time with Elizabeth. When she suggested again they plan a ladies' night, Kelly earnestly agreed.

She texted Eric at ten a.m. *U ok?*

Yeah. Home. Thx.

She refused to make the previous night real by asking any other questions.

~~~~~

Dale met Eric in the driveway with a urine test. Eric told him he would fail and Dale offered two options: rehab, or find somewhere else to live and work. Eric agreed to rehab and was waiting for Dale to take a shower and give him a ride.

He wasn't worried about detoxing, the two pills that night were the only he'd taken since he'd moved in with his parents. He was happy to get away, maybe get off some of the medication. It was a chance to start a new life where Charles wouldn't be haunting him. Where he could be a good father and, maybe, some day, husband.

He pulled up Joey's number, still saved in his phone, and sent a text, even though he knew there wouldn't be a reply.

Charles gone. Forever. Ur welcome.

~~~~~

Ben called Kelly around two in the afternoon, during the final championship match. She let it go to voicemail. *"Hey, Kelly, just wanted to let you know before you saw it on the news. The barn by that house near Grace caught on fire last night. Burned to the ground, but there was no other damage. Nothing suspicious, just some kids with a bonfire that got out of control. We should have gotten all that scrap wood out of the garages, it's like we left them kindling. The mine's fine, but we need to talk about putting a fence up.*

Otherwise, nothing to worry about, I just didn't want you to see it on the news. I do have some good news, but I'd rather tell it to you than your voicemail. Give me a call when you have time. Have a good weekend."

~~~~~

Jordana's team won the whole tournament. At the pizza place afterwards, Kelly felt sorry for the high school waitress trying to corral twelve pre-teens and their parents and siblings, but it was fun watching Jordana with her friends.

"Kelly, I'm so glad you could join us," one of the moms said. Kelly tried to remember who she was, but no name came to mind. "It must be so hard, being a single mom and having such an amazing career."

Kelly smiled. "I do my best." She braced herself for the coming "Minnesota Nice" insult disguised as encouragement.

"You do awesome," the other woman said. "Jordana is lucky to have you."

Kelly blinked, surprised. "Thank you."

"Let me know if you ever need any help. I don't think I could do it all on my own. Heck, I can barely do it with my husband's help. We all need each other."

~~~~~

After Jordana settled into bed that night, exhausted from the adrenaline of the games, the sugar crash after all of the celebratory junk food, and running around the mall with her friends, Kelly sat on the couch with a bottle of wine. It was probably too late to call Ben, especially on a Saturday, but she decided if he didn't want to talk he wouldn't answer.

"Hey there," he said. "I'm glad you called."

There was something in his voice—or maybe it was the wine—that warmed Kelly, sending calm all the way down her spine. They were going to need to reevaluate their relationship once the mines were open and everyone wasn't watching them so closely. If Ben wanted to, of course. "I'm sorry it's so late. I was with Jordana and her friends all day."

"No problem. I just wanted to tell you the good news. Our final permits came through at about nine o'clock last night. Grace can resume full operations Monday. Whiteside should be open by spring."

"That's amazing!" Kelly raised her glass in a one-person toast.

"And I hope I'm not ruining your Saturday night by talking about work, but we've also gotten the go ahead to expand into the Wanless and Woodbridge tunnels. We want to announce at the beginning of the year—or maybe right before—like *Merry Christmas, we're giving the Range hundreds of new jobs!*, so I want you guys to get in there and get your samples right away next week. We've got a press conference Monday morning, and from there I'd like to have a meeting with your team to discuss the expansion."

"Sounds great." She didn't mind talking about work on a Saturday night, she honestly loved her job. And knowing they'd won the fight and things were moving forward...it was a small victory to add to Jordana's. A good day.

~~~~~

The email came from Eric a few weeks later. Kelly had checked on him a few times, short phone calls, and he'd actually sounded really good.

It's time for me to get out of here. I got a place over by Fargo and will start a small landscaping company there. Dad's going to step back in in Rapids. I'm close enough I'll be able to see Matt a couple of times a month. If all goes well, I may get split custody in the next six months. I can't keep leaning on Mom and Dad. I've got to try this on my own. Thanks for your help and friendship."

Jordana went skiing with Sarah's family in the Upper Peninsula during Christmas break. Kelly was enjoying the quiet of her apartment and had promised her mom they'd go to Minneapolis shopping on Sunday.

Saturday afternoon Kelly stopped and bought a new plastic shoebox, never taking her gloves off as she carried it from the back of the store and through the registers where she paid cash. She stepped on it a few times and rubbed the lid in the dirt so it wouldn't look so new, but was careful to keep the inside clean. In her hallway closet the Ruby Slippers were still in the cardboard box she'd hidden them in so many months before. She carefully pulled it off the shelf and put it on the floor next to the new plastic box. With her gloved hands she removed her towels, cradled each shoe and carefully transferred them from one box to the other.

They certainly weren't what they used to be, but they were still The Ruby Slippers.

Getting a key from Jim for the shaft at Woodbridge was a little harder than it would have been from Frank. Strictly speaking, she wasn't supposed to be there, but when she told Jim she'd ask Ben, he'd relented. She'd studied the plans and knew construction was scheduled to begin reinforcing the tunnels right after the new year.

At the site, she slipped covers over her boots, tucked the shoebox under one arm and grabbed her flashlight. This mine had closed more recently and had modern technology like garage doors that could close each individual tunnel off in the event of a fire or flood. They'd rusted and deteriorated though, it didn't take her long to find one that was stuck. The bottom was crooked and left an opening high enough to shove the plastic box out of sight.

When she left, she made sure the building door was locked securely and wiped the handle. Then she drove to Grand Rapids, had dinner with her parents, and slept in her old room.

~~~~~

A couple times a year a storm would stop over Lake Superior for several days, sucking up the lake's moisture and dumping it back on the city in fat, sticky flakes. Kids loved it, because it was the kind of snow that made the best snowmen, and they got out of school. The second Monday in January, the day the workers were supposed to go into Woodbridge, twenty-two inches of snow was dumped on the city, delaying the work indefinitely. Kelly worried a little about the shoes, how they would fare in the underground tunnel, but, mostly, she felt a weight had been lifted from her. She had a new group of interns starting for the winter semester and, for the moment, nobody protesting her work.

*B*reaking news out of Grand Rapids tonight. It appears that the long lost Ruby Slippers have been found, hidden in an underground mine near Buhl, MN. Police say the shoes have deteriorated significantly over the years.

"I'm glad they were found," says former owner, Michael Shaw. "I hope they can be restored to their former glory."

There are questions over ownership of the memorabilia: because Shaw was paid a settlement, it appears the insurance company may get possession, although a representative says they have "no interest" in owning them. Several groups have come forward offering to take and restore the shoes, including the Judy Garland Museum, from which the shoes were originally stolen in 2005.

"This is now considered a closed case," said Detective Brian Richards, of the Grand Rapids Police Department. "While we would love to know more, the fact is, the statute of *limitations ran out several years ago. And, after this amount of time, finding new evidence is extremely unlikely unless someone voluntarily comes forward. Mostly, we are happy the shoes are back."*

Mark McDonald, the private investigator that had previously worked on this case, couldn't be reached for comment.

Kelly closed her laptop and took a long drink of coffee. Jordana came into the kitchen and put two slices of bread in the toaster.

There was a knock on the door, and Jordana was opening it before Kelly could tell her to stop. Mrs. McAlester was standing there holding a plate of fresh caramel rolls. "I felt like today was a good day to celebrate," she said.

"Celebrate what?" Jordana asked as she stuck her finger into the icing.

"You know, sometimes in life, you celebrate. Because you know things are going to be better from here on out." She winked at Kelly and set the plate on the table.

Kelly smiled. "Would you like a cup of coffee?"

"Yes, dear, that would be fantastic."

Author's Note

This book, like *The Thief,* was inspired by certain facts, but is entirely fictional. A pair of movie-worn ruby slippers were stolen from Grand Rapids, MN in 2005 and have never been recovered. The mines and cities mentioned are real places that did or do exist in Minnesota. There are currently companies exploring the idea of underground mining for copper and nickel in the state, although not in the areas (or the mines) proposed in this book.

Acknowledgements

To Leigh, Amber, Mom, Jessica and Lisa, thank you for your time, your insights and your editing. Craig Pagel and Frank Pezzutto, thank you for taking the time to talk to me about your jobs and the issues facing mining in Minnesota today. To the Minnesota DNR for the Underground Mine Mapping Project. Dad, thank you for talking through the mining issues with me, helping me figure out how to fictitiously shut down a mine, and for answering my random texts about hunting turkey. Thank you to my family, my friends and my mentors. I am beyond blessed with the constant support and help you provide.

About the Author

Amanda Michelle Moon is the author of two books in the *Ruby Slippers* series. *The Thief* tells the story of the real-life mystery from a fictional criminal's perspective, and *The Damage* continues the search. Both books are works of her imagination but full of facts and details of the actual theft and life in Northern Minnesota. A native of Hill City, Minnesota, she currently resides with her family in Minneapolis where she is working on two more novels. Her previous publications include articles for Pilates Digest and 2nd & Church and personal essays for Radiant Magazine. Read more at www.amandamichellemoon.com.

Made in the USA
Middletown, DE
10 May 2015